the Beautiful ones

THE BEAUTIFUL ONES
Copyright © 2002 by Kim Dulaney
All Rights Reserved
1st Edition

No part of this publication may be reproduced, stored in a retrieval system, or transmitted in any form or by any means, electronic, mechanical, photocopying, recording or otherwise, without written permission from the author. This novel is a work of fiction. Names, characters, places and incidents either are creations from the author's imagination or used fictitiously. Any resemblance to actual persons, living or dead, events, or places is entirely coincidental.

For information, contact the publisher.
Unique Expressions, Inc.
P.O. Box 11869   Chicago, Illinois 60611
e-mail: readme4000@aol.com
1-888-README4
www.readme4.com

Jacket and Book designed by:
j. sakiya sandifer
(www.stgrafics.com)

ISBN 1-891636-12-X

Printed in The United States of America

Acknowledgements:

Thanks to everyone that has ever read anything I've ever written. You make it possible for me to live my dreams… You give my life purpose. Thanks for peeking into the window of my soul without casting stones. I appreciate you!

Angie, Cookie, Doris, Felicia, Mae-Mae, Quintina, Rosalind, DeShonda, Kweisi and **Mel**, thanks for open ears.

To my editor and pen pal, **Isaac Perry**, the writing wizard, thanks for your support and camaraderie. Congrats on your new book deal!

Sakiya, thanks for being sooooo efficient and for working the late, late night shift (my time of day).

To my **Trinity Church Family**, thanks for feeding me… in more ways than you know… Bread and butter are a delicacy when served with your love.

To **Emmitt, Sam** and my brother, **Todd,** thanks for helping with the manly things.

Mr. Bingo, believe it or not you can win without playing (smile). **Secret,** close your mouth, you're drooling. Thanks for half of something when I thought there was nothing. I think I'll be okay now ♥.

Special thanks to -

My biggest supporter, **Santha Vonay Dulaney** - thanks for believing in miracles.

Andrea Moody thanks for consistently nudging me to branch out and for walking with me as I try.

Tracey, my sister, thanks for keeping it real and making it plain.
You all are a hell of a support system!

Mom and **Dad**, what can I say? Thanks again… and again.

To my sunshine, *Maya* and *Kendel*, thanks for every day. You two light my fire! You keep me keeping on. You are angels. Thanks for delivering God's messages! **I LOVE YOU!!!**

Finally, thank GOD for *thank you's* and black shoes!!!

This book is dedicated to
all those with gold shoes in dusty shoe boxes,
atop high shelves in dark closets...
and to those who wear them openly
because they have no closet in which to hide them.

In loving memory of Cathy and her "Smiling Eyes"

Part One

Intentions

1

Smiling Faces

"Lets play *Wanna Be*. And I call first."

"You always call first, Lila."

"Well when you think of it, you can call first. Okay, okay. I wanna be **Ms.. Carmen.**"

Lila held her head high, stretching her neck as long as the breathe she used to say the name 'Ms. Carmen.'

"That's not fair Lila! You always call first and you always pick Ms. Carmen! You know that's the smartest and the best woman in the world!"

"Well, I'm the only one who can really be Ms. Carmen. I don't want to get married. I am the fanciest girl in the whole wide world... of all the girls my age. I'm tall. I wear pretty clothes. When we play *Claim It*, I pick the best cars. I like to draw, and most of all, I don't care what people say about me!"

"Lila, you're a cheater! You think you're better than somebody! You get on my nerves!" Michelle wiggled her head, neck and body all at the same time, as if trying to line up the pieces of a jigsaw puzzle.

"Whatever," Lila replied as she stretched her neck a little

further and added a slow and smooth batting of her eye lids. "Now, who do you wanna be?"

"Mrs. Jenkins then!" Michelle snarled with attitude.

"OOHHH, you got a fat stomach, too many bad kids, and your husband won't let you go nowhere." Lila teasingly replied. "Unnnn, I can't believe you picked Mrs. Ladonna Jenkins."

Michelle stared at Lila blankly, embarrassed to have fallen victim to her tricks again.

"I shouldn't have even played. Ain't no way I could top Ms. Carmen."

Michelle plopped her chin between her palms as she steadied her elbows on her knees. Just as Lila prepared to stand and strut her royal Ms. Carmen-ness, a clicking noise came from the driveway. Lila and Michelle fixed their eyes in the direction of the noise. Within a couple of seconds a woman with a baby hoisted on one hip, an overflowing gym bag and burgundy colored imitation coach duffle on her shoulder, a pair of bright red, too-tight capri pants with red, strappy, leather-look sandals, appeared in the driveway. She was followed by a small toddler who seemed to almost miss the ground with each step he took.

"Hi, Mrs. Jenkins," the girls said in harmony.

"Hi, girls," Mrs. Jenkins snapped as she loaded the children and her bags in the car. "Are you supposed to be out here at this time of day? Don't you have some homework to do or some dishes to wash or something?"

Before the girls could respond, she continued.

"You have too much spare time. Why don't you both go and read a book or something?!"

Sensing that Mrs. Jenkins didn't really want a response,

the girls waited patiently until the car was completely loaded, Mrs. Jenkins and all, then in harmony once again, the girls spoke.

"Bye, Mrs. Jenkins."

"OOOoooo, I think she heard you Lila."

"She ain't hear nothing. And if she did, who is she gonna tell? She'll be too embarrassed because she knows its the truth and so does everybody else. Everybody but Michelle No Taste Buckley." Lila smiled.

"You get on my nerves, Lila. I'm gonna stop coming down here... just like my Grandma said, you don't know how to play with nobody."

Michelle stood up and started down the stairs stomping as hard as her short, little, shapeless legs would permit.

"You are no Ms. Carmen. You gonna be one old, lonely, empty, short - I mean *shalla* girl when you grow up."

She shuffled towards her house, three doors south.

"That's just a shame," she mumbled, finding comfort in her grandmother's speech presented to her just two days earlier.

"Whatever." Lila sighed a deep breath of satisfaction and turned and went into the house.

****

"I remember that day like it was yesterday. Everybody wanted to be Ms. Carmen. I never understood what that was all about. What was it about Ms. Carmen? That must have been, what, at least ten years ago? You should have seen little Ms. Lila come strutting in that door. I couldn't wait to call you. A daughter of mine, wanting to be you? Who would've thought?"

"That was funny. We laughed all night. Lila was such a snooty little girl, I didn't even know she liked me."

"Yeah, she liked you. Everybody liked Carmen. That was when you were rolling. I'm talking big-ballin. You and your black Corvette?"

"And the red one?"

"And the shiny black BMW? I loved that car. And the matching hair colors."

"I looked good, though."

"Yeah, you did. But you were far from a role model. I never understood why they all looked up to *Ms. Carmen*. Chile, you were a trip. When I called you to tell you about Lila and Michelle's little talk, you had just come back from a weekend getaway with Clyde, remember? Clyde the guy who played for the Bears. The married guy. The dark guy from the south who -".

"Yeah, Peaches, I remember. It was *my* relationship, do *you* remember?"

"Yeah, and remember you'd just got back from with Clyde, Tyrone was on his way over and Nelson sent flowers. Five minutes later and the deliveryman would've handed the flowers to Tyrone himself. I gotta tell you, I was wishing he would've caught a red light or something so I could have seen your smooth ass slip out of that one."

"You sure do love telling that story, Peaches. The thought of me being jammed up just makes you happy doesn't it?"

"Not really. Actually I just like studying people and their lives. Life is so interesting to me. People's perceptions and stereotypes amaze me. There just isn't any justice. Ladonna, the square ends up a broke down, desperate woman of ill repute. Lisa the tramp ends up landing a millionaire as does selfish, evil-ass Amanda. Sweet, caring Kenya ends up with Joe the whore. Spring's spoiled ass winds up a streetwalker..."

Carmen interrupted. "I've always wondered what you say about me. How would you sum me up Peaches?"

"Aw, honey, yours is something else. Ms. worldly, cool mama, Carmen winds up at home raising children, **alone**... being the role model for young women... with yo **wild ass!!!!** How in the hell do you pick disco mama, star-studded beau having, sex master wanna-be to head up a character building class at the local church? Can you tell me that? Honey, if they knew like I know, they'd be avoiding not only your church classes but the whole church neighborhood when you are up in there. I'm telling you one of these days that place is gonna burn down! Just spontaneous combustion - poof!"

They both laughed..

Peaches continued. "No, I really want to know. Answer that one for me Ms. Inspiration."

"They say you can't teach what you haven't learned. By that prerequisite I guess I qualify."

"Hell, you are overqualified if that's the case. Doctor to the tenth power." Peaches laughed as she continued, "PHD, or some shit like that."

"Come on now Peaches. I know you're not trying to judge nobody. A professional, gold-digging, pseudo psychic who can't even get her own shit right. Talking bout, 'just watch! Just watch!' And can't see nada! Can't see that fake-rich ass, wish-trust-fund having ex-husband of yours!"

Peaches laughed as she shook her head.

"Talking bout, 'they are giving me such a hard time. I'm going to eventually have to get an attorney to free up my trust fund.' NOT!!! Brother living in the hood talking bout his mama don't want to free up his trust fund. Yeah right?! You couldn't see that?! Just watch! Just watch! Damn blaring neon sign."

"Okay, Okay! I'm done. You done knocked my psychic power off track now." Peaches continued to laugh.

"I bet I did." Carmen smiled. "We all bought a few skeletons. I ain't ashamed of mine. Everything I've experienced has made me who I am today. Girl, I keep it real with my students. I don't claim to be Polly Purebred. You know my motto, 'ain't no life without some living.' But my purpose and goal is to let them know what excess will get them."

"I'm just joking with you Deacon, Dr. Carmen. Your secrets are safe with me."

"What secrets? Sugar, ain't no shame in my game. That's you all's problem. You want folks to believe you were born on Sensible Street. I think if all of these so called successful people would put their pride to the side and share some of their experiences it would help to guide others around some of these roadblocks. I'm talking about some real shit. Not that fake, 'Oh I once did something a little like that.' The real stuff! Without shame. Tell how bad it was so that people can see how good it can get! Look out now!"

"Oh, shit! Here she goes. Come on Reverend Clincher... Reverend suck em up. I once sucked a mighty one... almost choked the hell out of me... taught me to watch the size of things I suck on..."

Peaches laughed.

"Sounds important to me." Carmen said. "Might save a life or something."

"You gonna teach the little church kids that too?" Peaches teased. "No, really, I'm just joking with you. I know exactly what you mean. I wish someone would have told me something to keep me from some of the mess I've gone through."

"You know what I'm saying?"

"YES, I DO! That's what you should do, Carmen. Spread your dirt around town and get rid of all those fake, pretty thoughts people have in their heads about you. Just don't tell none of my shit! And don't let my daughter in your class." Peaches smiled.

"Why would I do a thing like that? When she has such a great role model like yourself to shape her and mold her?"

"Oh hell, why'd you have to go there? Forget it! Sign her ass up! Now!!" Peaches and Carmen laughed.

"Say Carmen, since we're talking about misconceptions and whores and everything, what was the thing with you and Spring? Come on, come clean. Was she like, giving you lesson or tips on man pleasing or something?"

Carmen sat quietly as Peaches continued.

"I mean she was a whore so I guess she would know some secrets, huh? At least she should." Peaches smiled. "I'm just concerned about you. I've always wondered what you could possibly have in common with her. Why do you keep ties to her?"

"We all know she was a whore, Peaches. You don't have to state that whenever you mention her. You wouldn't like people to mention negative things whenever they speak of you, would you? I don't think so. I mean *all* of us have something bad that could be said about us. So, you should remember that when you're judging folks. Spring and I were friends. Just like you and I are friends."

Carmen hesitated. She thought about how untrue that last statement was. Peaches was an acquaintance she'd known for years, not a friend. She'd met Peaches through Tyrone, her children's father. Peaches was Dino's girlfriend. Dino was Tyrone's cousin. Peaches wasn't the type of person Carmen would have as a friend. She was rotten. She was a troublemaker. She was a jealous hater who couldn't be trusted.

Carmen was aware of several times when Peaches had betrayed her. She'd spread rumors about things of which she had no knowledge. Stuff she assumed. Stuff she wished would somehow cast a shadow over Carmen's reputation. Stuff she thought could remove that damn halo from Carmen's head. That time when Carmen traveled to Orlando to hang out with Rodney, the NBA player, it was Peaches who'd asked Tyrone, "How was the game in Orlando? Is that stadium really as nice as they say? You know I can't wait until they tear down our old Chicago Stadium and build our fancy new place. Is Rodney really seven feet tall?" She had later claimed it was just an innocent mistake. She said when she heard Carmen was in Orlando with Rodney, she'd assumed Tyrone had taken her.

Yes, Peaches was rotten to the core. So rotten that it hadn't even surprised Carmen when she'd heard about Peaches and Tyrone. During one of her many breakups with Tyrone, one of his friends who had a crush on Carmen for years told her he'd heard a rumor that Tyrone had slept with Peaches while Dino was stuck out in LA. Dino was a struggling actor. He had gone to LA in search of work. He was really struggling financially. Peaches and Tyrone were supposedly working together to raise money to send him, when one day, as rumor would have it, it just sort of happened.

Carmen had tried to just write the whole notion off as a guy feeding her bulljive because he wanted to get her in bed. But in her heart she knew it was true. When she thought about it she remembered the day Tyrone had come home claiming that he and Peaches had a long talk and they cleared up some old things they'd thought about each other in the past.

Prior to that day Tyrone hated Peaches. Following that day, once the "air was cleared," he said he realized he had misunderstood her. A few years later, after Peaches and Tyrone's cousin had an argument about him being seen double-dating with Tyrone and a couple of hoochies, in anger, she had supposedly confided in a friend, telling the whole story. Her version of how Tyrone wasn't shit. How he'd taken advantage of her when she was distraught about his cousin. Well, of course, that friend told a friend, and that friend told a friend, and well, you know how it goes. Ultimately, it got back to Carmen.

Carmen was pregnant with Tyrone's second child when she first heard. She had thought of confronting them, but she felt her own guilt for dating the friend of Tyrone's who had told her of the incident. But from that time on, she and Tyrone were never to be the same. She sort of pitied them. She realized she didn't fit in their world. She'd felt so bad about her times with Doug, Tyrone's friend, that she almost told Tyrone herself. At first, in her own way she felt she'd paid Tyrone back for the Peaches incident and so many others, but then she realized that in effort to keep up with Tyrone she was shaping herself into someone she didn't want to be. Someone she couldn't respect. So she started on a campaign to change Tyrone and to get back to who she was. When she realized that wasn't going to happen, she left. She and Tyrone were basically done way back then. The rest was just going through the motions for old times sake.

Carmen stared at Peaches' *smiling face* as she thought about the fact that to this day Peaches and Tyrone were unaware that she had knowledge of their little rendezvous. And so, there Peaches sat, "concerned" about Carmen. No. Definitely not. Peaches was not a friend! Spring, now that was a friend. Peaches was just someone Carmen had known for a long time.

Carmen spoke. "Actually Peaches, what Spring and I talked about really ain't nobody's business."

"I mean, I was just asking. You get all sensitive when it comes to talking about her. It's like you are obsessed with making people think we were all the same, when, in actuality, no matter how you look at it her life was different. Then you go and risk all of your money on making her dream a reality. I just don't understand you when it comes to that girl. You wouldn't do that for me. Or for anyone else that I can think of. At least, I don't think so. Like I said, Carmen, I'm just concerned about you. You really aren't yourself. I talked to Tyrone. Tyrone says he doesn't know what's going on with you. I mean, what's up with you two? What's going on with that?"

"Well, actually..." Carmen's mind instinctively began to formulate an answer. Within a split second it had processed the inquiry, searched it's own database for the most appropriate response and issued the command – **Charge!** The words sharpened their edges, mounted up, and proceeded towards war with every intention of battling until the enemy was slain. Fortunately, Carmen caught the bloodsuckers just in time. They were right there, right on the tip of her tongue. A millisecond from landing their first blow which was guaranteed to break Peaches' face. But it wasn't worth it. Peaches wasn't worth it. Carmen only had one more day to keep the secret. She wouldn't allow Peaches to cause her to stray from her plan. She'd wait until tomorrow. The scheduled time. The time she'd be with real friends.

Carmen smiled a sly grin, like a playful cat whose lips are sealed because his jaws are filled with a terrified mouse, destined to be swallowed. She was pleased with the thought of Peaches being totally pissed once she realized Carmen sat right across the table from her, on the day before she made her big announcement, and never even mention one word about it. Carmen could imagine how Peaches would look when she heard the news through the grapevine. She'd probably look just like she looked a few years ago, when she'd taken Lila to the doctor for her six week check up and she discovered she was going to be a grandma, again, the second time, and this one was due right around the time Lila was to turn sixteen. Ladonna Jenkins had described that look vividly.

Carmen was overcome with satisfaction as she delighted herself in thought. News-worthy information to which Peaches was not privy? What could be better than that?

"That's not your business, Peaches, and I really don't want to talk about it." Carmen said nonchalantly.

"But it isn't just Tyrone."

Peaches was giving it all she had. She dug in deep. She wanted to know... needed to know.

"It's your mother, too. I ran into her at the grocery store the other day. She's worried about the way you've been lately? We're all just concerned about you..."

"I appreciate your 'concern', sugar, but I'm alright. Don't worry about me. I'm actually better than I've been in a long, long time." Carmen smiled her same sly, mouse-trapped grin again as she reached for the tabloid newspaper on the nearby table. "So, Jennifer Lopez got married, huh?"

2

Spring Reign Sumner

"God knows, if I had the money I'd give it to Carmen myself, Ace. If she knew I was asking you for money, she'd pitch a fit. That girl is so proud and stubborn. She thinks she has to handle everything by herself. I keep telling her everyone needs help - sometimes. I don't care who you are or how strong you think you are. Why, I even remember when you were trying to get started writing. You and your writing buddies would go out to Carmen's and eat, and have your little meetings. Carmen was single with Tyson all by herself, so money was sort of tight for her, but she'd scrape her pennies together to make sure you all had something to munch on while you talked about your books. Well, wasn't no books at that time, remember? Huh. That Carmen is something ain't she? She worked overtime to make ends meet for herself, yet, she found a way to get that money you needed to publish your first book. She really believed in you. Even when them big, fancy publishers didn't want to have anything to do with you. Now look at you. You have millions of people reading anything you write. All because that girl was willing to sacrifice her things so that you could get started. That's just how she is. I don't know why she won't let some of the people she's helped, help her. It's only right, don't you think so, son? I wouldn't even be asking you for help, but I know Carmen has always thought of you as a brother, and treated you like you were her own flesh and blood. You know what I mean, Ace?"

"Yes, Mrs. Trenton. So what happened with the art, the printer, the publishing and all of that?"

"Well, Carmen submitted a couple of paintings to have prints or copies made. She was going to have poems placed on the sides of the pictures. The pictures were beautiful. I wouldn't lie about that. Those pictures matched those poems perfectly. I had already told her I wanted a couple of them posters framed for my den. They reminded me of the type of pride we had back in the seventies. That young man Doyle does miracles with a paintbrush. He and that guy WAK. And Ulysses Jacobs. I ain't had a chance to meet him yet, but Carmen says he got a whole bunch of paintings that I would love. You know I like a lot of color. I don't like drab pictures. That Ulysses Jacobs, he uses bright colors. Anyway, she hasn't gotten the paintings, the prints, the money nor the writings back from those people. I told her there was something about those people that I didn't like. I told her that from the beginning. And you can ask her if I told her that long before all this came up."

"Who was the author of the poems? And why was Carmen publishing them?"

****

Spring. Spring Reign Sumner. She was Carmen's childhood friend and just like the season for which she was named, Spring was born of the need to buffer or merge two extremities. Deadly cold and too hot to handle. Instead of a water bag, that girl burst into this world out of a ball of confusion.

Her mother was a full-fledged, homemade bandanna-halter creating, 14" reinforced lime green lycra mini wearing, blonde pageboy sporting whore. Complete with "Please take me home" gold, glitter and Elmer's Glue enhanced stiletto slippers. A common Chicago Avenue "two dollar ho."

Her father was a wealthy businessman who fought hard to earn money, power, and prestige in a world far away from the less than humble housing project, that cradled him into existence.

In preparing his mind to make room for success he had to toss out some old to make room for the new. Even his own mama, sisters and brothers were sacrificed in his cleaning up of himself. I guess that's why he had so much available fire and passion. He was up there on his throne with no one to share his success. No real love, only fabricated love-like occurrences. The best occurrences his royal riches could afford. That would be Spring's mama.

Being the businessman he was, he realized he could get a better bang for his buck if he just bought the pregnant whore a house. She didn't know any better. She would think she'd struck gold. This way he could get occurrences as often as he liked and he could prevent her from filing for public aid. If she did that she'd probably give his name as the father. The child support they'd hit him for would be ten times the cost of a home. He'd just avoid the drama and the embarrassment. He regretted ever giving that whore his real name. He'd wished he hadn't been too tired to go and get his occurrence that night he paid her taxi fare to his home way out in the suburban gated community. If only Otis, the elderly guard had been working his regular shift that night. He wouldn't have even noticed her. But that damn wanna be robo-cop, Officer Daniels as he calls himself, just had to make the bitch sign the log. If she wasn't so damn good with his occurrences he'd just have a crackhead make her ass disappear. Aw, what the hell? Then he'd have to go through the whole process of finding another high-yellow uppity whore who seemed to somehow convince herself she wasn't the whore she was.

So, he fed her exactly what he knew she wanted to hear. Told her he wanted to take care of her. You know? His circumstances didn't allow for him to be with her as a couple, you know? But he said he had strong feelings for her, and liked her a lot. He thought she was special. She deserved the best life had to offer. That was all it took. With that he bought her and a $16,000, two bedroom, brick bungalow in a racially mixed middle-class neighborhood on Chicago's southside. Ironically, three years later he used almost the exact same words on Spring, his 3-year-old daughter, when he first introduced her to his occurrences. He stole Spring's dignity for a fraction of what he'd paid for her mother's. She never had a chance. No negotiating power. He was a big, hotshot businessman. In fact, he was too hot to handle, at least for little Spring.

He'd tell Spring she was all he had. It wasn't long until he was coming only to "see his daughter." Spring's mama would get dressed and leave the house. Spring would beg and plead to go with her mother, but her dad would say, "No, you don't need to go with her, baby. Dorothy's going to Oz. She's going looking for the wizard. That's why she wears those gold shoes," and he'd laugh a dirty laugh. As Spring got older, his visits got shorter and shorter. He'd usually show up right after she'd get home from school. That's how Spring developed her love for reading and poetry. She'd stay as long as she could after school, reading in the library. On Wednesday, the library was closed and he was sure to be there, at the house, in the living room sitting in the big green chair with the custom-made plastic cover, smoking his cigar. A thin paper bag from Gately's, TurnStyle or some nickel and dime store would be resting against his right leg. The bag and it's contents would be Spring's. That is, after his occurrence. Most often he'd leave right after his occurrence, before mama Dorothy got home. He was always in a hurry. He had "to go and see a man about a cat," he'd always say.

    Spring was never afraid to be home alone. In fact, when he'd leave, she'd go into her room full of things and play dress up. She'd pretend she was someone else, somewhere else. Sometimes she'd go far away to places she'd read about in books. Most of the time she'd pretend to be at Carmen's house. She'd even pretend to be Carmen's mom. She'd be cooking for her family, and she'd be clean underneath her clothes and she'd be a good kind of pretty, not the kind of pretty her daddy liked. Her trip would always get cut short when she'd hear her mother's voice calling her to come and see what she'd bought for her while she was out.

    Carmen was the only child in the neighborhood allowed to play with Spring. There was something about Spring's mama that didn't sit well with the neighbors. Though Spring's daddy was the only man ever seen visiting their home, there was something about their household that was mysterious and different. The mother dressed like a whore and she nor the weird man in the green Cadillac was friendly. They never participated in the block club meetings or block parties. They never even smiled or waved when the neighbors tried to speak. Plus, the little girl Spring was a different type of child. If ever there was rain the neighbors could look outdoors and spot Spring standing, sitting and once even kneeling, motionless as the rain washed over her. Strange.

Carmen didn't care. She thought Spring was fun. They played make believe together. They would pretend things in nature were their friends. They danced with trees. Spring recited poetry to an audience of dandelions. Carmen would hold sticks in the air to create frames around works of art she'd find, like a rainbow or clouds shaped like angels or perfectly round treetops with long slender trunks that she would swear was nature's portrait of that lady with the big fro', ummm...? Angela Davis, Spring would announce. "Yes, ladies and gentlemen. A portrait of Angela Davis by Mother Nature," Carmen would declare. Then at the perfect time a gentle breeze would blow applause through the field and the dandelions joined by all things natural would stand and cheer in appreciation of Carmen and Spring's talents. Spring loved Carmen for playing with her. Carmen was her best friend, her only friend. Even at seventeen when Spring had bought her own pair of gold shoes and set out to find the wizard herself, Carmen had not stopped being her friend. She lectured her for hours and even though that didn't work, Carmen never gave up on Spring.

That's why Carmen felt a pain in her heart years later

when she had to tell Spring, her "friends or habits" were no longer welcome at her home. That was after Carmen's son had answered the door to find the police staring him in the face while holding up badges and a search warrant. After the search the police had informed Carmen that her house had become a part of an undercover investigation when packages addressed to Carmen's home were intercepted. The packages were found to contain illegal drugs. Several packages from various days had been confiscated. Carmen was furious. She traced the timing of the packages back to a period of time when Spring and her shady looking man were visiting frequently. The whole ordeal was like a nightmare. Not only did Spring violate her trust, she violated her home. About a week after the search, Spring had tried to call Carmen to explain. She apologized profusely and told her she had no knowledge of what had gone down. She swore it was all Julio. Julio had set the whole thing up and was meeting the deliveryman there. She didn't find out about it until she confronted him after she heard rumors on the streets about Carmen's home being raided. Julio admitted to using the address and promised that nothing could be done to Carmen. He said the police would just harass her a little, but they couldn't pin anything on her. "Quit trippin," he had said. "Ain't nothing gonna happen to that scary bitch."

Six weeks later, after the heat died down a bit, Spring popped up at Carmen's home. She was moving and talking slow. As soon as she saw Carmen she began to shake her head from side to side as if trying to rid herself of the memory.

"I'm sorry C. I swear on my granddaddy's grave, I ain't know nothing about that. I wouldn't do that to you. We tighter than that. I would never disrespect you, your kid, your house, your momma, your mail..." Spring batted her eyelids slowly as she rambled on. "Man C, you can call the police. I'll tell them it was him. I'm not worried about him hurting me. He shouldn't have done that!" Spring jerked and stumbled backwards as she tried to get excited. Carmen grabbed her by the arm and held her until she was steadied.

"Spring it's not working, sweetie," Carmen began.

"Please don't call me Sweetie, C."

"Spring, this is not working. You've got to find a way to let it go. You are grown now. You can be anyone you want to be. Who does Spring want to be? Huh? What does Spring want to do? So, you gonna just let them win? What about Spring? Spring is beautiful! Spring deserves more than this. You hear me, Spring? Huh? Time out for excuses. Okay? You don't have to be out there. I know who you really are. Why can't you grab a hold to that Spring? The Spring that I know can do better than this."

Spring stood limp as she began to sob.

"You got any gold shoes, C. Mine are a little too small. Had em' since I was three. They're wearing out," she said as her tear filled eyes momentarily snatched all understanding from Carmen's being. After several moments, Spring broke the silence when she grabbed scraps of paper from her purse and shifted her attitude to one of reacquainting with an old friend.

"I got some good ones, C. I wrote these the other day while I was sitting over by the lake. Listen to this."

She sat on the porch railing and began reading poetry from the slips of paper. Carmen followed Spring's lead and rested her exhausted body against the concrete wall. The night was long. Spring read from folded napkins. They cried. She read from notepaper with various names of hotels printed at the top. They cried. She read from torn box tops and from scribbled on, magazine pages. And through the night they cried and revisited that place from their childhood. The place they both knew and loved. Spring couldn't force herself to leave. By sunrise, she sat second step from the bottom with her head resting on Carmen's knee, fists full of scraps that she was tired of trying to piece together.

Seven years later, one rainy afternoon in early spring, Carmen received a visit from Ms. Dorothy. There had been a quick, small funeral. There was no time to contact anyone. Spring's body had been found in an alley on 75th Street a few blocks west of Halsted. Her throat had been slashed. She was stripped of all her clothing except for a pair of faded goldtone, strappy sandals. When they found her it had been raining for three days which is about how long they estimated her body had been there. The rain had washed away all but traces of her makeup and it had faded her gold shoes.

Ms. Dorothy's foot jerked back and forth tapping the stiff air as she spoke in a cold empty voice while providing the details of Spring's death. Ms. Dorothy wore black shoes. Black smooth-soled stiletto pumps.

Carmen sat in a daze as she listened and imagined Spring, alone, helpless, trying to pull it together.

"She would have died anyway. She had AIDS," Ms Dorothy spat. "She wanted you to have these. I barely ever spoke with Spring these last couple of years. The only time she would call would be to give me your new address whenever you moved. Then she'd send these letters. She asked me to save them until she was gone then to give them to you."

Ms Dorothy handed Carmen the cardboard box, which was covered in daisy-printed paper. Carmen sat wondering how Spring could have known where she moved to. She never left forwarding addresses.

Ms. Dorothy continued.

"I don't know what got into Spring these last few years. She was not in her right mind. She had taken to making up stories and talking crazy."

Carmen opened the box. Affixed to the inside of the top was a mirror with a picture frame drawn around it. Next to the mirror in a small velvet pocket was a tiny charm made in the image of a pair of high heel gold shoes and a note on a torn piece of paper. It read:

"Ladies and gentlemen, in this mirror is the greatest work of art known to mankind, Ms. Carmen Trenton, by none other than God Himself. C thanks for being you. I leave you my gold shoes. I know it's safe to leave them with you. You outgrew the possibility of ever having to wear them a long time ago. I want you to have them to remember me by. Afterall, I won't be needing them anymore, you'll be happy to know, I found the Wizard (smile).

Love Always, Your Sister, Spring Reign Sumner
Peace.

****

You know Ace, I know my daughter well. I've watched she and Spring's friendship over the years. I must say, it seems to me like Carmen is closer to the girl now than she was when she was living. Carmen seems determined to use Spring's story and her writings to effect lives. She had a couple of artists create images to capture the essence of Spring's poems. She took the paintings, the poems and a deposit of $15,000 to a local printer and prepared to save the world or at least exhaust herself trying. Looks to me like she's taken on more than she can handle this time.

3

PO-KE-NO!

"Getting married?! When? Where? TO WHO?!" Renee spurted out the string of questions without pausing for answers.

"Why?" Rudy added sarcastically.

They all sat around the table overwhelmed by Carmen's announcement. No one suspected this. They were all asked to meet at Paje's, a trendy restaurant on Chicago's north side of town. Carmen said it was a mandatory meeting. She had something very important to discuss with everyone. There was no discussion. Carmen had started the evening off passing around the boards preparing for a game of Po-Ke-No. There was the usual: a dollar per board, per round, and fifty cent per board, per round for the four-corner pot. Everything seemed normal except, why Paje's? Why tonight? Why mandatory? Wagering was usually reserved for second Saturday, every other month at the home of one of the members.

The atmosphere began to make some of the women uneasy. The candles in the center of the tables had already burned pass *quick announcement* level and were easing into *casual relaxed chit-chat* mode. The flames of friendship serenaded the hot wax causing it to blush and settle snuggly in it's space. The waitresses and waiters worked the half-empty room without a sense of urgency as if they were cousins serving aunts and uncles at Big Mama's house. The room was dimly lit with the exception of track lights which hung low in single file lines that almost split the row of tables perfectly down the center. Everything was smooth, slow and easy. Almost too easy. Although seven of the thirteen ladies were entrepreneurs who could basically set their own hours, the other six had to punch clocks between 5:30 and 7:30 am. Some had kids to pick up from sisters and parents houses. Several had dates. One had to get home to try to double-up on birth control pills since she'd missed last night's dose and it was two hours pass her daily scheduled pill-popping time. This just wasn't a good time for games. The women began to grumble.

Carmen managed to keep her cool. When she'd had enough of their complaining and whining, she had just said in a very nonchalant fashion as she shuffled the cards, "I'm getting married."

Then she'd called the first card for that round. "Ace a spade."

She placed the card face up on the table, and called the next card.

"Six a club."

They all looked around the table scanning each other's faces, searching for confirmation or clarification as to what they thought they heard. Carmen never looked up.

"Seven a heart."

Now they all stared at Carmen.

"Yes, I said seven a heart," Carmen said. As she raised

her eyes to greet their stares she broke into a smile.

"Po-Ke-No," she said slowly, careful to pronounce each syllable.

The ladies continued to stare in silence. What was really going on? First of all, Carmen didn't even have a board. And did she say something about marriage a second ago?

"Seven a heart, po-ke-no, I win tonight, baby, baby!" She popped her hand up in front of her face to reveal the diamond engagement ring she'd slipped on without their noticing.

"Bling! Bling! For your aaassssss!"

Sharon was the first to speak, "Ain't that a bitch!"

Then Emily blurted out, "Hell, naw!" She said it so fast at first it sounded like she was speaking in tongues.

That's when Renee rambled off her string of questions to which Carmen had responded, "New Years Eve, my house." Then through a huge smile saturated with sweetness she added: "Marcus."

Carmen looked into the faces of her friends as she read the minds of each and every woman seated around the table. Their thoughts were like images projected on a mega-movie screen and Carmen could see them clearly – even without her glasses...

4

Box of Business

I know they are tripping on this. Twenty years with Tyrone and I up and marry Marcus in just five months. I know exactly what they're thinking. Look at them sitting around this table in shock. Maybe I should have told them one-by-one. I just wanted to avoid the gossip. I would have had to answer the same questions over and over. I hate to even imagine what they are going to say about Marcus. Poor Marcus, I put him through the ringer those 3 years of being just buddies. He was always saving me... from some no good rat and myself. Today I thank God for him. But I remember when I cursed God for making me love someone so worthless, with no direction or future and most importantly, no money.

****

I cried like a baby after the first time we made love. He was my friend and my hero but he was broke. I knew to keep him far away from the goodies. I adored him, otherwise. I knew if I ever broke down and served him the goodies it would be all over. It was the day before I was to leave town. I was extremely depressed. The printer had gone out of business with my money.

I had orders but no product, which means I couldn't expect any money from my publishing for a while. I had no money to hire attorneys to get my money back. I was so determined to get Spring's work published that I broke my own rules of business. I let emotions rule me. I gave the $15,000 deposit, Then, before the printer completed the first phase, I gave them the second installment. They said they'd ran into a couple of problems and needed more funds to get my order out within the next month. Well, the order was already two months behind and I was losing money. So I figured, why not? I had worked with them on a couple of other projects and although they were slow their quality was good. Plus, I understood the plight of the small minority businessman and figured this was my way of helping them. Then I got the call asking for the balance. I reminded them that contractually I was not obligated to pay the balance until I received the product. Then the whole lie started to unravel. They had not printed anything. They had completed pre-press work only when, out of the blue, their presses were repossessed. As a result, they subcontracted the final process of the job through a fellow printer with whom they were friends. The only problem was they had to give him half the money up front and they didn't have it. It amounted to about the same as the balance due on my project. I was angry and disappointed but I was also without options. Almost all of my money was tied up in the project with this company. I could use the little money I had left to start a legal battle and lose my shirt or blouse while we fight it out or I could just give them the money this time, get my product and swear not to do business with them ever again. It wasn't like I could start a whole new project. I barely had any money left.

Plus, this project was one that was going to be blessed by God. I just knew it. Spring's writings are powerful. I thought it might have just been some sort of test to see how bad I really wanted the project to succeed. I was wrong. I was wrong in a big way. There I sat, with $5700 a month worth of bills. No product and no money.

In addition to that, the IRS was attempting to charge me $85,000 extra for what they perceived was unreported income. In actuality a friend in the NFL had given me funds to purchase art and accents for his home. Several of my celebrity friends had enlisted me to shop for them. I was considered broker to the stars. Now this particular butthole was acting flaky. I needed a letter from him verifying that the money he had given me was not a gift but was for things for his home. I couldn't find his rich ass. He hadn't returned my calls and his agent's office told me they couldn't give me a letter until I spoke directly to him. I think he was somewhere in Hawaii or something. While he was in Hawaii the IRS was in my ass. Mind you I hadn't included any fees for my five months of shopping nor had I added a real profit onto his prices. He was my friend. Saved his damn-near 10 million-dollar-a-year ass a minimum of $100,000 and now it was going to cost my broke ass $85,000. Go figure.

The whole ordeal got really ugly when a girl that had a thing for the guy, The NFL Player, embellished some things to get what she wanted or needed from him. She used me and my IRS issue in her mess. I couldn't believe it! That caused the whole thing to be drawn out longer and longer.

Ultimately, she got what she wanted and I was left with people looking at me cross-eyed. I couldn't believe she'd lied like that. I thought of calling someone to set the record straight, but I didn't have the energy nor did I want to perpetuate the drama. All I wanted was the IRS off of my ass.

I couldn't understand why she felt she had to lie. It was unnecessary. He would have helped her. Moreover, I wondered why he believed her. I was crushed. But that wasn't the worst of it. Believe it or not, after a while she came back around and expected me to behave as if nothing happened. She never offered an explanation or anything. She just smiled a girlish, *I'm back* sort of smile and expected me to embrace her. Hell no! I don't think so! The thought of me braking down and forgiving her made me want to run to the other end of the earth! I would have moved to West Hell to get away from her and from Tyrone's ass, whom I had just broken up with. Again.

But it didn't stop there. My grandma used to say, "Baby, when it rains it pours." And she was right. On top of all that, I was dating a wealthy, self-centered, fine-ass bastard who thought that I should be happy to see him when he happened to make his rounds through Chicago.

Honey, money makes life funny.

My car note was a month late. My car insurance had been canceled about three months prior. My mortgage was two and a half months behind and I was just about ready to say screw it and take up residence on one of those grates downtown on lower Wacker Drive. I was dealing with all that and two children by my damn self. Losing my natural mind.

That was until my buddy Marcus called. He was going to stop by and put together a bookcase I had bought a while ago. Marcus was always doing something for me. Shoveling my snow, cutting my grass, fixing or installing something, bringing me something, moving or shipping product for me. Marcus was my angel. But Marcus was broke. Handsome, but broke. Sweet as pie, but broke. Sexy as hell, but broke, broke, broke. If he could just hit the lottery or inherit a fortune, he would be all mine, I thought to myself. I watched his muscles flex as he put pressure on the screwdriver he used to drive that screw into my bookcase in my bedroom. He was so strong. I remember thinking to myself how much I adored him.

After he put my bookcase together, he took me to get my oil changed because he didn't like the way my car sounded. That was right on time because I had to drive all the way to California the next morning to try to sell a few paintings and hopefully get enough money to keep my house out of foreclosure. That little $20 he spent was like $2,000 to me at the time. Then he ran a couple of errands with me and agreed to meet me back at my house to give me a massage so that I could relax. No big deal. He had given me massages several times before. He liked to make me feel good he had said. He enjoyed seeing me relaxed. He was good, too. He would make me feel like all of my problems were oozing out of my body with each caressing stroke. I often got massages, but Marcus's massage was more of a loving caress. A gentle stroking. Marcus loved me and I knew it. I felt something for him, but I was determined not to face it. Whatever it was. Whenever I felt it coming on and growing stronger I would distance myself from him. But this day I was weak. I didn't feel like fighting. I just wanted Marcus to rub away my problems and my fears then go on his merry way.

I showered so that I would be nice and fresh when he

arrived. I loved to have lotion rubbed into dry, slightly ashy skin. I put on loose fitting shorts with one of those white, men's tank tops. You know the ones southern folks call wife-beaters. I was loose and free waiting on my buddy. No underwear of course, because it won't be a problem for Marcus, he doesn't get excited easily. Well, about thirty minutes later I was in heaven.

Marcus was rubbing me and telling me how he still wanted me and he said he was a patient man and that he understood me and he would wait and take it slow and I would be his wife someday, if God would allow it. And he was stroking and talking slow and smooth in perfect rhythm with his stroking and I was relaxed and free. I knew Marcus meant what he was saying. He was consistent. Not once had he wavered or changed his thoughts or feelings about me. Not once in our three years of friendship. But Marcus knew like I knew, that I would not completely let go. My buddy. That's what he was and that's what I needed him to be. Until today.

It had been awhile. First he kissed my knee. Gently. Then quickly blended it with the massage. Almost quick enough for me to think he hadn't done what I thought I felt. Then he kissed my navel as he caressed my stomach. Then he began to massage my breast. He did it in a business as usual type of fashion but I could hear his fingers talking to me. I opened my eyes without moving my body.

"Beautiful," is all he said.

I know it sounds fairytale-ish and it was. He began to rub me again as if he understood that it was not okay, yet it was o.k. I relaxed into my thoughts wondering how I got to be so determined to have a man who could offer excessive security. I always ended up not liking them. Self-centered millionaire after millionaire. I laid there enjoying Marcus's touch wondering if all this security was really necessary. Shit, after all, how much did a girl like me need and was there anyway Marcus could possibly get it? All of a sudden my body filled with fire. Marcus had wandered down. I don't know what he could have been looking for but he had found his way into my private sea and Marcus could swim his ass off. Not only was he a good swimmer but he had already found the buried treasure. This brother was a hell of a navigator! My goodness! I began to feel something. That something that I always avoided with Marcus.

"Marcus, Marcus, Marcus," I managed to whisper.
He pretended that he thought I was disciplining him and he kissed the waves he had created and he stopped swimming and resumed his caressing. He spoke to me in casual conversation as if he hadn't just damn near drowned in my soul. He looked at me in my eyes as he casually conversed about something which I cared not know.

"I want you to be comfortable and happy," he said.

I interrupted. I knew the game he was playing and it was turning me on. I already told you I was exhausted and had no strength to fight. What was I supposed to do?

I interrupted, "Do that again."

"What's that?" he asked as if he didn't know what he had done and he rubbed my back just the way he had done prior to my request.

"No, the other thing," I said in a low psychotic voice.

"What?... You mean - " he lifted his body over me and widened his eyes, "Suck your pussy?" Oh, shit! That was it. The moment. I was outdone! I knew I had to find that brother a job. He could do landscaping or sum'n. I could scrape up on a lawnmower, a rake, a shovel. Hell, a snowblower, paintbrush... SOMETHING!

You know, I just talk that fancy, lady-like bulljive. Truthfully, most women I know like a little bad boy, a little raw, rough freak in a man. Don't hurt me... don't get beside yourself and get physical, but a little friendly, dirty language never hurt anything.

After I had felt good for a little while, I told him we had to stop. My kids would be home any minute. He understood that, though he wasn't too happy about it. He knew he had impressed me and would probably be allowed to come back that way again. Once he was gone, I cried. I had the audacity to call on God and ask him how he could be so unfair as to take most of the qualities I truly desired and put them in him. Marcus, the broke handyman. I was mad at life for being so real. I was mad at myself for playing with Marcus one time too many. Now, I was facing one of my worst nightmares. I had fought it for quite sometime. I had told myself he was probably awful in bed or had an extra ear growing out his ass or something. But now I knew him completely... and I loved him. Needless to say, I spent the rest of that evening on the Internet and the phone looking for a job. A job for Marcus.

Then the other day, exactly five months later, he showed up at my house grinning like a fool, bugging me about recounting the shipment of masks I had recently received. I felt something was wrong because Marcus seldom talks bad about anyone. "I don't trust those Africans," he had said. As I rambled through the box recounting masks, just as I had figured, there in the middle of the box was a gift for me. A small blue Tiffany's box. That's where he had it. I later found out that he had sold his old pickup truck to buy me the type of ring he felt I deserved. And he went through a lot of mess for that little blue box. He had bought the most inexpensive item they had at Tiffany's, returned it, and kept the box. My ring had actually come from that fancy pawnshop right off of Michigan Avenue. It's worth $10,000, but it only cost him $3,000. Four carats, total.

Three center stone and one total for the baggets on the side.

Marcus is always working something out. Just last night after we laughed about the ring ordeal he showed me his box of business. Believe it or not, he owns two rental properties and has about $8,000 in bonds his father left him that he has never touched. He said he thought he should share that information with me since we're getting married. He didn't want to start this marriage with secrets or lies. At least his heart is in the right place.

****

"Carmen, would you like another glass of Kool-Aid?" Darcy the waitress asked.

"Yes, please," I replied.

As I thought about my Marcus, I looked around the table at all these women with curious eyes and confused faces, women who had respected me and lived vicariously through me and my millionaire escapades with hopes that I'd be their connection to "the good life" and I considered telling them about Marcus' box of business. Then I decided I didn't need Marcus' box of business to validate my choice. That little blue box was enough of our business for one day. Then I smiled and proudly proclaimed, "He loves me, y'all, he loves me."

No one spoke, but I could hear the narration. The reels were rolling and the picture was clear and crisp as I watched my life's movie play out in their minds. They each directed their own version, their own way...

Part Two

Dinner & Silent Movies

5

Talking Hennessy

This is unbelievable! After all these years of being single she's actually gonna do it again. Tyrone won't believe it. Hell, I don't believe it. That stuff with Spring effected her more than any of us could have imagined. And Marcus bought into that? He's known her for a few years. I would think he'd know she's just emotional about Spring. This escapade won't last forever. Forget prenuptials, I hope he got a warranty. She's gonna be bored with him in 90 days. I know Carmen. Just to think, all this started because of a worthless whore that nobody even paid attention to.

****

Summer 1999

Stereo thumping Prince's, *1999*.

"Yeah, tonight we're gonna party like it's 1999! Drink up ladies. That Prince is a mother ain't he? He knew way back when that 1999 was going to be a pivotal point in time. A time for change and new beginning," she said as she poured what appeared to be 3 or 4 shots of Hennessy into each persons already partially filled glass.

"Oh, I got more Cristal for you bourgeoisie broads up front. Don't worry, everybody's getting blistered tonight."

After about an hour and a half of watering down everybody, she had suddenly reached towards the table and scrambled to pick up the colorful box that had gone unnoticed until that moment. She then popped up enthusiastically and while smiling a loaded smile, she declared, " This is it y'all. Today is the first day of the rest of our lives. This will be the day we all will remember."

She carefully took Hennessy steps, high and a bit wobbly, towards the huge chalkboard in the corner that just seemed to magically appear when she was ready to take us on this journey she had planned for us.

"Okay, y'all. We're gonna do something profound today." She stood smiling, pronouncing each syllable of each word perfectly, just as an intoxicated intellectual would. We all looked at each other inquisitively. Where was she going with this and when in the hell was she going to get there?

"Okay, y'all ready?" Carmen batted her eyes repeatedly then continued. "Now this is a special group here tonight. Like a club or something. The purpose of this club is to make all of our wishes and dreams come true. We go'ne laugh together."

She was losing her grammar a little now and her words came slow-fast, if you know what I mean. They even slurred and ran together a bit.

"We go'ne cry together. We go'ne support each other however we can..."

Rudy interrupted, "Oh, yeah?," and smiled.

"Anyway, we can," Carmen responded, raising her eyebrows causing her already large eyes to protrude as if they were going to pop out. "Well, all except sex of course. But we got something for that, too."

I had to laugh at that. Alcohol has a way of bringing out truths. Carmen, Lisa, Renee and I had all thought Rudy fancied women. She had never actually said it, but everything about her was screaming it.

Lisa had choked on her drink when Carmen made the sex statement.

Realizing what she had said, Carmen just smiled and said, "Well, this group is about being real... and honest. It's all between us. Nothing said between us can leave us. Like they say what goes on in this room stays in this room. Now, if you think you can't hang with that, then you can scadoodle right now. It's been fun and we won't hold it against you or anything, but peace out."

She paused for a moment as if actually waiting to give someone a chance to leave, all the while knowing that sheer nosiness was going to keep each and every soul planted. "First rule: It's between us. Second rule: No harsh judgment allowed. We're here to uplift not to put down. Third Rule: Honesty. Next: You must share... and work with each other. If we are going to share burdens, then we need to share other stuff too. Next: No negativity. This includes but is not limited to gossip, jealousy, and yes ladies, MALE BASHING!"

That's when the crowd grumbled. "Huh? Whaaaat? You've got to be kidding. Well." Even Amy from the Cristal side of the room had let out a long drawn, ghetto-rooted,

"Sheeeiiiiiiittttt."

Carmen erected her body and stood blinking her eyes slowly.

"It isn't about men or women or none of that," she said. "This is about us fixing us. We've got to work on us before we can introduce the problems of the rest of the world."

With that she turned and began to write on the chalkboard. NAME: _____

"Now, who has a name? I haven't been able to think of one." She turned to face the crowd and swayed a bit.

"How about Drunk Asses," Sharon joked. Everybody broke out laughing, including Carmen as she fell backwards into the wall, hands over her chest.

Jonay broke the laughter after about a minute when she suggested, "Women of Distinction."

"Women of Color" and "Dynamic Divas" followed that, and finally the name that got the Hennessy side fired up, "Intimate Indulgences of Intellectual Achievers." That one came from Miss Veronica. We now call her 'Missy.' Sharon gave her that name. Missy had recited that title as if she had actually put a lot of thought into it.

There was silence for about 30 seconds after she'd said it. Then, for fear of it actually being considered, Sharon had nodded in agreement and sarcastically stated, "Right, Veronica, That's a good one, that or maybe 'The National Association or Professional *Head* Administrators.' Either of those would be cool."

"Yes," Veronica concurred in her royal heiress. She didn't have a clue as to what Sharon was referring to. I almost pissed my pants! Carmen did piss her pants, though no one knew until months later. But that's another story.

Those of us who knew Sharon couldn't stop sniggling. Finally, Carmen looked at me and announced, "I think that's all the work we are going to get done tonight. What do you think, Renee?"

I just laughed and nodded my head. Afterall, I had left my keys under the mat and I was sure Big John was there for our 2a.m. SUMU session and if I was late he'd leave and it may have been a week before I could get him back where I wanted him.

But that was 98lbs ago. His fat butt had the nerve to make me last on his list of ladies. I did all the tricks hoping to persuade him to visit during the day. Can you imagine cooking fried chicken and macaroni at one in the morning? Cause Big John wouldn't eat leftovers and he wanted his food hot. So there I was cooking and tasting and sampling in the middle of the night, no wonder my diets didn't work.

Now, I don't care if he comes or not and I can't get rid of him. I'm not bragging. I'm just stating the facts.

Anyway, that was three years ago. That's where we started... that night at Carmen's. Seems like a whole different lifetime.

As we all gathered our things and filed out of Carmen's newly rehabbed, colonial style home in Chicago's inner-city, upper middle class Beverly area, Carmen stumbled onto the front porch and in a Hennessey inspired jovial manner suggested, "You all are gonna love it. I'm telling you. We are just going to make the good better. That's all. Here's to us."

She smiled and raised her Tupperware tumbler in a

pretentious manner that was uncharacteristic for Ms. No Frills Carmen.

Emily reached for the handle on her brand new Bentley and turned to face Carmen. With one hand reaching for the door she used her left hand to cock her wide-brimmed straw hat acey-duecy as she shot back at Carmen in agreement, "I don't know if it gets any better than this, mama. You know we are the beautiful ones. Replies of, 'For sho', 'You know that's right' and 'All day' echoed through the silent night's air from different directions.

Yeah, beautiful ones. That's right. "So *Beautiful Ones* it is," Carmen exclaimed as she was hushed by her final kiss of Hennessey.

****

Renee took a deep breath and began picking through her salad for the fourth time since she'd decided she was done. She found a piece of egg and small square of chicken deep beneath the dry lettuce. She reluctantly ate them both then called to the waiter seated in the back corner talking with a lady friend.

"Excuse me. Can you come and clear this off when you get a chance? And I'd like another Diet Pepsi, please."

Then she picked up a napkin she'd used earlier to wipe her boot. She dropped the napkin in the center of what remained of the salad, hoping to cancel any possibility of continued nibbling. Just to be sure, she grabbed the napkin and touched it over the entire area of the plate while pretending to pick something from beneath her nail.

"That should do it," she whispered to her inner self.

Then she turned towards Sharon and asked, "Married? Can you believe this?!"

6

Roots

"I ain't mad at you, Carmen. Handle your business, girl. You couldn't have picked a better man. I wish you both all the happiness you deserve."

Everyone stared at Sharon with disbelief. Sharon, emotional? Everyone but Carmen that is. Carmen knew Sharon well and understood that she was just like a chawawa, feisty and always barking, but her bark was much worse than her bite. The most danger you could possibly face with Sharon was if you messed with Carmen. Sharon was very protective of Carmen. They had been through a lot together and Sharon knew that they understood each other. They had spent years shaping and reshaping lives together. They shared roots. At least that's what Carmen had confided in me. Carmen was very protective of she and Sharon's relationship. It was as if they shared a secretoath or something. As far as I know, I am the only person Carmen trusted with even snippets of their business. I guess it was because I'm her sister. But even I understood that there was a place in Carmen's world to which only Sharon was privy.

After all, it was Sharon who had stepped way outside of her norm and allowed, no suggested, that they tie the mattress and boxspring to the top of her less than one year old Mustang and drive through the city in broad daylight with one hand on the steering wheel and one hand out the window to balance the oversized beginnings of Carmen's first bachelorette pad.

She was even the one who found the ad for the discount store just up the street from the projects in an area where she'd dare not travel to under normal circumstances. Then they had struggled with those mattresses and that narrow hallway with that blood-sucking stucco mess on the walls. Why would they put that stuff on the walls? It was usually reserved for ceilings. But this was the ghetto. It was a really nice courtyard building with a quaint little one-bedroom apartment that was much nicer than the three-bedroom apartment we lived in with our mom, dad, three brothers and little sister over the cleaners on 63rd Street. Her new place reminded you of a scene from Eddie Murphy's movie Coming to America. It was like a diamond in a pile of shit. Well, maybe a cubic zirconia.

Carmen would sit in her car outside of the building and pretend to be occupied while she waited for the hoodlum looking young men to finally move their loitering away from the black wrought iron fence that surrounded her building. Then with key in hand positioned just right to assure a quick and smooth entrance, she would put on her hard, ghetto pimp walk and make a dash for the door. Inside was her pearl lacquered bedroom set with the gold trim that she had purchased from Sears, her gray and black striped sofa and love seat trimmed in black lacquer with her matching black lacquered coffee and end tables she had purchased for much more than they were worth from Renta-World, the black lacquered lamps with the gray shades and gold trimmed base that she had lucked up and got on sale at Ventures, her white microwave with matching white microwave cart/utility stand which was a gift from her mother, her perfectly coordinated ruffle trimmed towels and plastic flower-print shower curtain which Sharon had matched perfectly to the diamonds in the shiny vinyl flooring in the tiny bathroom, and most treasured was her huge boom box with cassette player and detachable speakers.

Yes, Carmen was rolling. At twenty-two she had it all. Sharon was so proud of her. She had committed herself to sewing all of her outfits for partying as long as Carmen bought the fabric. She understood Carmen had to pay rent and stuff and wanted to help out anyway she could. As a result, Carmen wore all tailor mades. You wouldn't have imaged that suede came in so many different hues. Every payday, Carmen would hit the fabric store on her lunch and by party time, which was about midnight, she would be glistening like the star that Sharon felt she was born to be. Yep, Sharon and Carmen were connected. Like peanut butter and jelly, hot dogs and pork and beans, red beans and rice... they were a team.

Sharon and Carmen had secrets.

Sharon was the first to know of Tyson. Carmen was engaged to Cedric when Tyson was conceived. Cedric definitely was not Carmen's norm. Cedric was attending church regularly. He could have easily qualified as a deacon with all of his churchly interaction. That's basically how they ended up together. It was as if Carmen thought she could erase her past dealings and be labeled an instant righteous woman because she was with Cedric, 'the good guy.'

Cedric was an alright-looking guy. He was somewhat intelligent. He had a good job with a good salary, especially for a young man his age. He took care of business. Cut grass, washed cars and did all the things Carmen was taught a man should do. Overall, he would have been a good catch. But Cedric had self-esteem and family issues that made him a nut.

Carmen was afraid of Cedric. All possibilities of love are negated when you are driven solely by intense fear. Carmen learned that lesson the hard way. She has often said if she were not so afraid of Cedric, she would be married to him today. Our parents have been married for forty something years and Carmen desired to have that type of marriage, too. She admired the things he stood for, but typical of a situation filled with abuse, she said he was stealing her will to live. She tells of one time when she was in the kitchen near the knives which he often used to threaten her. She says she looked at the knives and if it wasn't for her fear of not being accepted into heaven she would have done what Cedric had not yet found the courage to do and ended the ordeal herself.

Instead she just cried to God asking him if he didn't think it would be better for everyone, to just look the other way when it was time for her to take her next breath. She said she had cried uncontrollably and asked God to just take her from the situation. Within a couple of months God had answered her prayers. Not in the way she had thought necessary, but he had provided the perfect opportunity for her freedom.

In the meantime, Carmen had taken up with Tyrone secretly. Tyrone had been faithfully stopping by the salon hoping to catch Carmen there. No one could believe Carmen had actually broken all ties to Tyrone. But she had. That is until Tyrone lucked up and caught Carmen at the light on 79th street, one block east of the salon. Tyrone smiled and beckoned for Carmen to please pull over for a minute. Carmen had obliged. It had been awhile and Tyrone had been a good friend besides being her ex-lover. She thought it was innocent. But given the circumstances, any mature woman would have known to keep going. Carmen spoke with Tyrone briefly but left the encounter with a cell number, home number, address and pager number. Tyrone wanted her to have his info in case she needed to talk or anything.

The next thing she knew, Carmen was somewhere in the clouds counting snow flakes one by one on a late winter afternoon from Tyron's oversized bed. She and Tyrone's legs intertwined like pretzels as they lay at opposite angles, arms outstretched, hoping to solicit a magical breeze from the heavens from which they'd just returned. Tyrone gasped, "I can't breathe," as Carmen concentrated on pulling air long and deep into her lungs. She could feel her heart beating strong like thunder... racing. Not here. Not now. Though this was an ideal way to go, she did not want her body to be found here. Not like this. She and Cedric were to be married. She needed to relax and breathe and make it out of this place. She couldn't embarrass her family like this. She couldn't blacken her own legacy like this. She had worked hard to acquire and to maintain her good girl image and now that she finally had it just like she needed it to be... No, she had to relax and breathe. She couldn't die here. The thunder slowly turned into a drumbeat and later the tumultuous reunion celebration faded into a rhythm and ultimately eased into a gentle melody.

Carmen said it was amazing how much courage she'd

found. She knew Cedric would find pleasure in killing her if he knew she had now provided him with an excuse that would enable him to be understood or deemed reasonable in his actions. Carmen vowed not to ever see Tyrone again. She felt like such a hypocrite. Here she was attending church every Sunday, Bible study, Prayer Meetings, couples fellowship and young adults board meetings weekly and yet, she had just crawled out of Tyrone's bed. Yeah, there was no living left on this earth for Carmen. Subconsciously she deemed herself dead. She would have to just make it through the rest of this life and look forward to the beauty and fulfillment of Heaven.

Little did she know. God had other plans. He was the giver of life. He knew how much she could bare and for some reason he had decided that she could handle double that of which she previously owned.

Three weeks later she discovered that she had not left Tyrone's with a secret spark of life that would be buried deep within forever as she had thought. She had two sparks. One that belonged to her, that she would keep and treasure, and one that she would share with the world about nine months later.

His name was Tyson.

As a result of her shame, guilt and fear Carmen figured she'd better go ahead and have sex with Cedric. She wouldn't enjoy it, and she was sure this would be the last time she'd ever allowed him to touch her. Now she had a reason to live. She had a life inside her and she would do whatever she had to do, to keep it safe.

When she'd allowed Cedric the pleasure, she didn't move through the whole ordeal. She just laid there like the corpse she was. She had hoped it would be as bad for him as it was for her, but Cedric was excited and seemed to really enjoy himself. How? Who knows. I guess just like men and blow up dolls. Carmen was so sickened by the whole thing that immediately following Cedric's moment, she found herself hugging the toilet seat. Whether it was Cedric, or morning sickness that caused it, who knows? But, according to Carmen, it was late evening when it happened.

Carmen said she expected great things from Tyson. God planted him here smack dab in the middle of a storm so he must have had a very special assignment he needed to be handled. My mom says she knows his mission and he completed it the day he was born... that was to save Carmen's life. We all agree.

Sharon hadn't known of Carmen's secret meeting with Tyrone. No one knew. But she knew something wasn't right with Carmen. Carmen was a walking dead woman and yet, she seemed content with it. There was no life in her eyes, no smiles, no excitement but she had a newfound peace about her. Yep, something was seriously wrong and Sharon knew it. And when Sharon had suggested that if the child was a boy it should be named Cedric, Jr. and Carmen had cried and said "over my dead body," Sharon was not surprised. Then when Carmen had decided that she could not bare to live a lifetime of lies and deceit and when Tyrone kept requesting that she have a blood test despite her adamantly saying it was not his child, it was Sharon who stood by her side as she cleaned the skeletons from her closet.

But that was only one of their many secrets. Sharon could write a book about Carmen and vice-versa. They're blood cousins who share an intimacy greater than a husband and wife. They were cut from the same cloth. Planted in the same field. They had grown together and everyone knew their bond could not be penetrated.

 They were 'rooted.'

****

 Sharon sat very still, barely blinking as she stared at Carmen reminiscing. Then as she smiled and shook her head side to side, she said, "You are one crazy person and I want to be just like your ass when I grow up."

 Ironically, I was sitting there thinking the same thing and it must have been written all over my face. Sharon looked right at me and pulled me in as a co-signer.

 "You know what I'm saying Carla?"

 "Yeah, I'm with you. This one here, she's something else," I said.

 Sharon continued. " Remember when this crazy ass woman had that meeting? 'Butt Naked'?"

 All of us seated around the table smiled and shuffled, shifting positions as we recalled that emotional evening...

7

Butt Naked

"I think the problem is you ladies don't realize how fine you are." Carmen spoke with confidence as she called the '*Butt Naked*' meeting to order.

"On the paper provided I need each one of you to write a list of five things that make you attractive. I mean physically attractive. No, 'I'm nice, considerate, thoughtful,' stuff tonight. Tonight I want to know what makes you so fine. You get three minutes and everybody has to write down at least five things."

At the three-minute mark, Carmen, who had completed the assignment in about a minute, stood up and continued her preaching.

"I'm convinced self esteem is one of the major problems amongst women. We talk a good game, but do we really believe all that good stuff? We prance around proclaiming, 'I know I'm the shit. I'm a Queen. I deserve to be treated good. I love myself...' Is that right? I want to know about it then. Who wants to go first?"

"Well, since it's your show, why don't you go first?" Renee suggested. "I know you've probably got thirty things on your list."

"You damn right, sugar. Ain't no thang. I'll go first." To

everyone's surprise, Carmen didn't have a list. She had a whole poem. She started teasingly in a rap type rhythm:

> "I'm tall and sort of lean
> with a look that's oh, so clean
> I was blessed with the perfect bend at my hips
> which coordinates heavenly with my afrocentric lips
> my hair is a gorgeously natural thang
> and when I walk I've got this cool, sort of captivating swing
> I've got this smile that brightens my own day
> with a teacup of tits that are sexy in their own way
> I don't desire to make you like what you see
> But please don't hate, when I'm loving me."

"And you know this man!" she howled in Chris Tucker fashion.

The room went wild. I was in tears. 'This fool is crazy' is all that I could think. Then she goes around the room in raw form.

Renee watched carefully with one of those, *this bitch thinks her shit don't stink* smirks on her face.

I knew that Carmen meant exactly what she said but the good thing about it was that she wanted each and everyone of us to feel the same about ourselves. She had spent our entire childhood luring me into similar types of games and activities. Eventually, I found responses that would be deemed acceptable, and I committed them to memory. I think I rehearsed those answers so much that I actually began to believe them.

"Black is beautiful," Carmen would say.

She spent years pounding that into my head. It took a while for me to believe her. One event changed my mind and ultimately my life. My cousin was dating this guy named Richard. Richard was this fake fancy guy who worked at one of those big banks downtown. Once, I went to my cousin's home to pick up a pair of black silk shoes and a set of luggage. I was taking a trip to Alabama to be in a wedding. A friend that I went to high school with had just put me in her wedding and I was left breaking myself to participate in an event that I hadn't even planned on attending. Well, the bride requested that we all wear black silk pumps. I'd spent $275 on a dress I could never wear again and I wasn't about to spend $100 more. I would have worn yellow shoes if I hadn't found a pair to borrow. I don't know why I put myself through all of that. I should have just said 'no.' Anyway, when I went to pick the shoes up from my cousin, I happened to overhear Richard talking about Carmen. It was a hot day and the front window was open with a fan in it. He was talking about how Carmen wasn't all that attractive to him. He said he actually thought she was kind of homely. You know? Not polished. She needed to leave them cornrows alone and stop pulling her hair back into that little afro puff thing. This isn't the 70's. She would never get anywhere in life looking like a homely "flower child."

I was pissed! I rang that doorbell and when Janice, my cousin, opened the door I walked straight past that punk without saying a word. When he insisted on bugging me to try to get me to speak to him, I cursed his ass like he was yesterday's trash. He looked surprised and said he didn't know what my problem was, but it was apparent that I had one. I told him to kiss my black ass and get a damn life. As I struggled to open the door, I added with as much energy as I could, "half curl wearing, white boy wanna be, broke ass, butt kissing trick," and stormed out the door. I had hoped he would say something back. Give me a reason to light into his little frail ass. He didn't. He just sat there looking nervous, like a chick or something. I was mad as ever.

I left there and went straight to Carmen's and told her what happened. I'll never forget her reaction. She reached over and gently patted my knee while smiling and said, "Never, ever let me be your issue. I know you love me, sweetie, but believe it or not, not everyone feels the same about your darling sister. Different people like different things and different looks and its okay. I have a hard enough time handling all of the ones who find me irresistible. God has to save some for others, Boo. You've got to get some. Janice has to get some. Like I say there's some for everyone. Hell, even Richard's ugly ass has to get some."

And with that, Carmen burst into a hearty laugh that tickled my soul. We laughed so hard we cried.

Through tears she added, "He may think I'm ugly, but he surely thinks I'm special. He spent all of that time discussing little ole me. We gonna end this shit right here, cause..." She giggled and struggled to catch her breath. "... that little freak ain't worth not one more second of my precious time. Bout' to make me late for my dinner date. Now, lets talk about him. He's fine. And he likes him some ugliness. Got a fine friend who might like a little ugliness too, if you want to come along."

She held her hand up for high five and we fell out laughing.

"Ain't that cute," she said as she collected herself and grabbed her bath towel. "Carla, you cursed him out girl? Did you tear his ass up?" She giggled. "I guess you are old enough for me to tell it to you plain. I've had problems but men ain't one of em'. Your sis..." Carmen peeked her head out of the bathroom door, "is always on overload. I only use one gun at a time, if you know what I mean. But I've got an arsenal full of some heavy artillery, stashed in this mother-so-and-so, baby girl." Carmen smiled and widened her eyes. "Naw, don't ever let me hear of you bothering yourself with that kind of mess."

She closed the door, turned her music on blast as she always does when she showers, and began her usual off-key crooning. There was a sense of freedom in the air and I knew Carmen meant what she said. From that point on I've been concentrating my efforts on my type: Strong men who prefer strong black coffee, no sugar, no cream.

****

So, when it was my turn, I gave my answer and passed the little game without comment or criticism. When it was Sharon's turn, Carmen asked, "O.K. Sharon, what do you have?"

Sharon responded with, "Well, I couldn't think of five things because I never really thought of myself as being fine. I mean, I know that I've got a nice ass. At least that what they tell me. I've got nice arms. They're not where I want them to be, but we're working on them. My hair is O.K. It has seen better days, but it's O.K. . That's about all I could think of."

"Really? Well, that wasn't too encouraging," Carmen

said. "Nothing is quite right. I just need to tell you that you are on some bullshit. Look at you! God puts his mighty hands to work and creates a masterpiece and it isn't good enough for Ms. Sharon. I could see if you've let a few things get out of hand and you want to get that back under control, but what about you and your God given beauty? You are a fine motherfucka! God hooked you up! What about showing some appreciation?"

"Well, I mean my nose is a little wide and..."

"Thank God! He blessed you with that shit because that is how he wanted you to look. Where is the standard? Who made the rules? If your nose isn't so wide that your breathing has to stop when you need to listen to someone, then you're straight."

It took a moment for me to understand that one, but I got it.

"You are somebody's dream. Their beauty queen believe it or not. And they don't know anything about you being sweet and caring. Trust me. Why is that so hard to believe?"

Renee interrupted.

"But Carmen, why is it that you say it's okay to be different when it comes to features, but when it comes to size, you feel totally different. Not that I really give a damn what you or anybody else thinks. But you just gave this big nice speech to Sharon about accepting differences, yet you think it isn't okay for a, let's say larger person..."

"Okay, okay. It just isn't healthy to be obese. That isn't my opinion. That's fact."

"But who..."

"Let me answer the question Renee. If you have a huge person that's really, really big..."

Renee moved around on the couch and attempted to sit up straight, which shifted her weight from the sunken cavity her wide behind had quickly created, to the fresh pillow directly next to her. Carmen was relieved that something had caused her to give that one pillow a break. She had been sitting there concerned that it may never be able to fully expand again. But, she couldn't bring herself to ask Renee to sit in a chair.

"Like I said, if the person is really big to the point of their weight causing health problems or even a not so big person who is miserable with all the extra weight, then it isn't acceptable to me. Let me tell you this. I saw on Oprah that one out of every two women will die from heart disease. One out of every two! So if your weight causes you to be unhealthy or unhappy, yes I have a problem with it because it's stealing your life. If you are big and you feel it is who God would have you to be, and you are able to celebrate yo' fine self and you're healthy, then I don't have anything to say about it."

Carmen's head tilted slightly. Stress lines appeared on her forehead as she attempted to filter the words that were seeping into the porous processing chamber of her mind. Like a sponge long after the mess is clean, her mind retained traces of dirt from spills caused by Renee's carelessness with her filthy mouth. Negative trash spewed from between Renee's lips on a regular basis.

"Now if you're a person who says 'size doesn't really matter', yet the truth is you're bitter, and feel bad about yourself, so you feel the need to search me to find and make me aware of what you consider deficiencies, so that I can feel bad too, and we can be on one - *all of us are just so screwed up accord...* then I have a problem with you and your problem because you're making it my problem. You know what I mean? Face who you are. If you are fat, then you are just fat. We all know how we look, who we are, what we consider our strong points and weak points... and if you are comfortable with it, cool. If not, change it. Life is about being the best you that you can be. I hate to say it but sometimes it requires a little effort from you. Sometimes it requires a lot of effort from you. Anyway, what's on your list? We've had this talk before and you know we won't agree so let's just move on. What's on your list?"

"Well, I know I'm fine. I mean some people might have a problem with it, but as long as I like it and my man loves it, I don't give a shit about what some little malnutritioned, bony ass, jealous wenches think about me."

"Okay, so what does your list say, Ms. Proud to be Big Mama?"

Renee enunciated each word carefully.

"I've got a nice nose. It's keen and cute. My eyebrows have a perfect arch and they're really nice. My mouth isn't all big and sloppy. It is small and feminine. My feet don't have any corns. I've got wide feet, but at least ain't no corns like some of these girls who walk around with sandals knowing their feet are tore up. And I'm okay with my body. I'm big boned so I will always be a little thicker than most, but it ain't like I'm fat or nothing."

Everyone in the room was silent.

"I mean that's about it." Renee pursed her lips together and attempted to stretch her neck before sinking back into the sofa.

The room was silent again. Then Carmen asked, "So who's next?"

"Wait, wait." Amy interjected. "You mean we are just going to let that go. I thought this group was about honesty. You want me to believe that you don't think you're fat?"

"Who says what fat is?" Renee questioned.

"Maybe the scale? Maybe the tag in the back of our clothes? Maybe the third or fourth serving of food on our plates?" Amy was serious and everyone knew it. In an otherwise playful group, not one person laughed or snickered.

Renee was offended. She was hot and it was obvious.

"Amy you ain't too small yourself. Just because you've lost a couple of pounds, now you think you are the fat judge? If you don't like how I look then don't look at me. And I promise I won't look at you. It ain't like you're easy on the eyes anyway. I don't sit and talk about that nappy-ass hair on that swollen-ass head of yours, do I? At least I can loose weight if I choose, but you are stuck with that damn pear-shaped head of yours."

"See, why are you angry? It wasn't even about all of that. My head is my head, and you're right, I was born with it. Were you born with all that lard choking your heart? You're right, you can do something about it. That's what makes the situation so sickening. You can get angry if you please, but if we are going to be real about it, then I can't sit here and listen to you talk about how three hundred and fifty pounds is just big boned." Amy was the sophisticated one of the bunch. You could never really be angry with her because she was a straight shooter. She followed all the rules in life, and just about every move she made was in direct correlation with an anticipated result.

Renee knew Amy was right. That's why, though Renee had the sharpest tongue, and could have cut Amy to tears, she just responded with, "Whatever."

That's when Carmen introduced the exercise that took the group to another level. She went to her kitchen and grabbed the old trusty liquor bottles, which she housed beneath the sink with her cleaning supplies. She insisted that everyone drink up. Lisa made the comment that if we kept this up we wouldn't need The Beautiful Ones, we could forgo the travel across town and just go to our respective local AA support groups. Once boozed up, Carmen asked everyone to go upstairs into her bedroom. It was crowded in there, and hot and clammy. She opened her closet door and stood in front of the full-length mirror that was on the inside of the door. We could see her image in the mirror and she could see us.

Carmen stood there for a minute before she finally spoke.

"At thirty-something, if I can't look in here and like what I see, then I've got a problem. No one is perfect by society's definition, but God has made in us, some beautiful women. You must come to believe that. To embrace that. To know it as fact. Or we won't be able to teach it to our children, our men, or this world as a whole. Until we are truthful and confident and comfortable in our skin... we will never reach our God given potential. Now, look at me."

She stood there staring at herself. Then she took off her t-shirt. Then her oversized jogging pants. She stood there in her inexpensive sports bra and what she called her period panties, which were a little large for her already wide derriere.

"As a child I was made to feel that my knees were

unattractive. These are called knock-knees I was taught by the children on my block. There weren't a lot of opportunities for me to be teased. I had a lot of brothers and sisters plus there were three other households filled with cousins of mine in the neighborhood, so people seldom messed with any of the Trenton's. And my mother didn't allow us to play the dozens or fight amongst ourselves. That was totally out of the question. She taught us that there was enough negativity in the streets that we would have to face. We were to band together and help one another survive and be safe against the world. If one person fought we were to make sure it was a fair fight. And if someone was getting the best of us in what started off as a fair fight, the next child closest in age to the one being pounced on was supposed to step in and fight the battle for the losing relative. Then, if all else failed, we all were to muscle up and fight as one unit. And we had better not lose the fight either. So, as a result, there were things that I didn't know about myself until someone was lucky enough to slip something in on me. *Popeye* and *knock-kneed* were the names I heard a couple of times. Once, this little boy who liked me, called me, libba-lips. I never knew exactly what he had said. Now, as an adult, I realize I was lucky. If that was all they could come up with to say about you back in my day, in my neighborhood, then that meant you must have been fine. The funny thing is, it was usually the child considered the most unattractive who picked out differences in others and labeled them ugly. Later, in life I was told that I had bedroom eyes, and I found that the same things that made me different as a child, made me different in a positive light as an adult. Bedroom eyes and luscious lips were what the men who were attracted to me loved most. The knock in my knees was so slight and so well camouflaged it went unnoticed. My knees became my own treasure when I realized they were in direct alignment with my bow hips that seemed to capture the world's attention and afford me the opportunity to have my pick of the male species. Also, they went along with my double-jointed body that enabled me to be as delightful in the boudoir as a contortionist is to the circus. Think about it, without these knees right here," she grabbed the thickness that protruded from the inside of her legs just beside her knees, "I wouldn't be able to run along the lakefront or walk into a play, a museum, a concert. I couldn't jump up to block my son's shot in our basketball games. I couldn't push myself to the edge of a heart attack, just to beat my daughter in a friendly game of double-dutch jump rope so that I could brag about how I've still got it for months to follow. I guess I'm saying, if any part of me were different I wouldn't be me. At least, not as *I* know me. And I've spent some time with this old girl."

Carmen stood proud, with her hands on her hips.

"I've grown to really like her. As a matter of fact, I love her."

The rest of the night was spent introducing each of The Beautiful Ones to themselves and the rest of the group.

"Come on, Renee," Carmen had said with her arm outstretched.

She waited in front of the mirror as Renee reluctantly made her way across the room. Renee took her own sweet time stepping over and around the ladies who were packed in that room like sardines. After a few moments, with her arm draped over Renee's shoulder, Carmen turned Renee to face the mirror.

"You *are* fat, Renee. Come on now, I know you know that. Not just big-boned. You're correct when you say that you're pretty. But just imagine if you would be willing to work with God, instead of against him. Has anyone ever told you that you are entitled to more than one blessing? You can be pretty and in good shape and educated and so many other things, if you are willing to accept God's gifts. Take your shirt off for a minute."

"Naw, I'm not gonna do all that. I know how I feel about me, and all your dramatic acting ain't gonna change that."

"Well, why not just do it. We're all women. We don't want you. Girl, we see the same things you see everyday."

"Because, I just choose not to."

"Are you embarrassed?" Sharon asked.

"No, I just don't feel that I need to expose myself to you all so that you can tell me how I should feel about me."

"Well, this group is about exposure, Renee. Nobody's picking on you. We're exposed every time we have these meetings." Emily's patience with Renee was wearing thin. She continued, "If we are just going to deal with everybody else's issues and run from our own, then what's the purpose of this group? Look at this shit!"

Emily grabbed a handful of herself, which seemed to claim it's own special compartment positioned near the lower half of her stomach.

"I know I'm out of control." She stressed the KNOW. "I don't know how in the hell this got here."

She shook the pouch uncontrollably. "I just woke up one day and it was here. Sort of like an unwanted guest. I been hinting to the fact that I don't want it here, but I have yet to get off my ass and kick the son-of-a-bitch out."

Renee suddenly snatched off her top unleashing her insecurities. "Now what?"

"Now..." Carmen spoke gently, cautiously, releasing each word as if it were a piece of rare, priceless crystal. Carefully... delicately, she fostered the smooth landing of each word, each syllable. "Look at yourself."

"Okay, I admit I could use a little tightening up, but I don't desire to be itty-bitty."

Renee stood there looking at Carmen. She had actually only glanced at herself in the mirror for a hot second, then she had turned to look at Carmen.

"Sweetie, you have a ways to go before itty-bitty is used to describe you. Don't worry about that. What are you shorty, 5'4" ? It just isn't healthy."

"Says who?" Renee barked.

Then Jonay challenged, "If you are so content Renee, then why are you taking ten to twelve colon cleaners a day? You do know that's an addiction. You can ruin your body's natural ability to process waste."

"And weekly colonics? Why?" Leah questioned.

"See you're so smart that you're dumb. If you check with any holistic health professional you'd know that not only is it smart to clean out your system, it is necessary. And you know what? If I was popping Xenadrine like most of you in here, I'd probably be thin as a rail too."

"Enough said!" Sharon yelled as she rambled through her purse, grabbed the half empty bottle and reached over and stuffed the bottle into Renee's purse. The bottle peeked out just enough to show its name... Xenadrine.

"Now! That problem is solved so let's move on." Sharon waved her hand to the side.

Jonay spoke again. "Well, Renee, all you really have to do is cut down on your carbohydrates. You know? Pasta, rice, bread, potatoes. And cut down on your fat intake. Drink lots of water and do some simple exercises on a regular basis. I do two hundred jumping jacks a day. 100 in the morning. 100 at night. Twenty lunges and maybe 50 sit-ups. That's it. I take my lunch to work 4 days a week and I walk everyday after I eat my sandwich. Oh yeah, I walk from the train instead of catching the bus. It's only 4 blocks. That may sound like a lot of stuff, but I'm telling you it's easier than it sounds."

"Well, that's good for you. I know what to do if I wanted to lose weight. Like I said, I ain't trying to look like I'm starving. That's y'alls thang. I'm cool with me."

"Okay. Y'all heard the woman," Sharon yelled. "Now can we move on?"

Well, we learned a lot that night. Some offered tips on accenting what you already have. We shared the latest on where to get the best bargain on padded bras, girdle panties, body shapers and yes, padded panties, too. When we talked about hair and hair weaves, it opened the door to lots of secrets. There was so much fake shit in that room. Hair, breasts, permanent eyebrow arches, sucked and tucked guts, arms and thighs... You would have been surprised at who had what done. Carmen proudly said that she had never had anything done, but she took the number of the discount surgeon in Mexico just in case she ever really needed it. It was a weird night. Women showed off their works and their marks or lack of marks. Until that night I had thought that stuff was reserved for white women or rich minority women who'd wished they were white.

The night ended hours later after everyone had shared stories of who they knew had what surgeries or fake hair or colored contacts. I think just as many men had been mentioned as women. Even with regards to plastic surgery. That was a long night. I don't know if our talking for hours or Mr. Hennessy was responsible for Carmen curling up with a pillow in the corner of the room, but when the sun came busting in through the mini-blinds at about 5am, Sharon had scrambled to her feet an announced, "We ain't got to go home, but I guess we got to get up outta here."

Everyone was slow to gather their things. We had bared our souls in that room and it felt like a safehaven. We wished we could just freeze time and stay there... in the moment. I left there feeling good and bad. Bad because the world is just too fake. Good because, now I had an excuse to stop busting my ass trying to keep up with the video queens, models and actresses. I could be proud that I was all me and after that night any woman that looked too good to be real, probably wasn't, even if she really was.

Later, everyone noticed that Renee was eating less and slowly but surely the pounds began to melt right off of her. She was feeling herself, too. It was obvious. Honey, Renee was wearing sleeveless tops and dresses that actually dented at the waist. No one said a word until finally about six months later, at a barbecue with an extravagant buffet at Emily's house. Renee was in line behind Veronica and Veronica suggested that she try some of the frappe, which had just been set out on the table, and Renee replied, "I don't think so, Sugar. I've got to protect this girlish figure of mine."

Everyone laughed as Renee added, " I know you trifling bitches done noticed all the weight I've lost, but it's okay. Y'all ain't got to say shit. I know I'm looking good."

At that Veronica had set her plate on top of the plastic cake dish and gave Renee the tightest squeeze that her frail little arms could manage.

But Renee wasn't the only one changed that Butt Naked night. We all got a glimpse of the light at the end of the tunnel and each started on our individual journeys towards a brighter tomorrow.

****

"Carmen's getting married. I guess we did something right." Carla said as she took a sip of her apple martini. "So Carmen will I get more nieces and nephews out of this deal? What's in it for me?"

Carla's question caused Emily to choke on her champagne. Emily dabbed a napkin on her lips as she thought of the possibility...

Nothing but the Truth

Well, what can I say? I hope it works out for her. I don't know how it's gonna work but I hope it does. She's a nice girl, a little weird, but nice. And Marcus is a good guy. I've known Marcus since I was six. He lives right down the street from my mother's house in his mama's house. I just hope she don't try to make him something that he ain't.

Marcus is nice. He's a sweetheart. Actually, a couple of times I thought me and Marcus were gonna hook up. We that cool. He does so much stuff for me. I hope she ain't marrying him because he fixes stuff for her. I tried to tell her that he fixes stuff for everybody. That's just who Marcus is. She's talking all this mess about him being consistent and all that. That don't mean nothing, really. She ain't special. He do the same things for me, and he's done them for others I know too.

Just last month, Marcus had obviously had a little nip and was telling me all his business like he has so many times before. He told me about him loving him a woman with some junk in the trunk. Now, I ain't saying he was hitting on me or nothing but there always been chemistry between me and Marcus. I know if I would have meant it when I offered him my bed, he would have took it. Like he say, he like em' wit a lil junk and you just don't find more junk than this here. Otherwise, why'd he even bring it up?

Hell, Carmen is more hips than anything. Her trunk ain't nearly full if you know what I mean. There might be a blanket or a picnic basket in there. Maybe. And barely that. So he sho wasn't talking about her. When I thought about it, I ain't never seen Marcus with nothing but fuller-figured women. Never. Not once. I hope she knows what she getting into. All I can say is if it ends up screwed up, at least I tried to tell her. That's all I could do.

I mean, I could have had Marcus. He's a real nice guy and everything even though doesn't have anything. He needs the right woman by his side to bring that potential out of him. I'm sorry, I just don't see Carmen as that woman.

Marcus needs somebody like me. That's really what he needs. I don't know why we never hooked up.

When we shared that bottle of Moet a few years back, I noticed Marcus leaning his head way back looking up at my mirrored ceiling. I knew he was probably losing control. Somehow he was able to keep his dick from getting hard. He must've been pacing hisself so he wouldn't let me see that I was affecting him. And I ain't even phony or fake. I knew what he must've been thinking so I crossed my legs and kind of twisted myself just enough so that my cheeks peeked out beneath my big t-shirt. I had on my leopard print thong but I must admit, all this ass had that little string playing hide and seek.

I smoothly slid my foot down and touched his arm right beneath his shoulder on that big muscle. I know his ass had to be hot because I had the killer pedicure. My nail tech had just put this Hawaiian scene on that big toe. She had just finished about two hours before Marcus came to unclog my toilet. Well, that's what I told him I needed him to do. But really, I just wanted to surprise him.

I couldn't believe he had said 'no' when I asked if I could show him exactly what he was missing. He just stared at the ceiling, smiled, and said, "Naw, I'm go'ne have to pass on that one."

About a year later when we was in the same setting again, he had explained to me that we cool friends and he ain't want to mess that up. But truth be told, if I really, really wanted him, I could have been had him a long time ago.

Just like I told her it wasn't gone work with the rest of em. It ain't gone work with Marcus either. Carmen needs a older man. I tried to tell her that from the beginning. Just like I been trying to tell her about Marcus. She don't want to talk about him since they done got all serious and stuff. Now they done got engaged. Well, since she ain't want to listen to nobody, I guess she gone get what she deserves.

9

The B Side

Well, well, well. Would you look at Ms. Chocolate Temple. I wonder if Marcus knows who he's marrying. Carmen or Chocolate Temple? See, we had this thing, right? On the first Friday of each month, we would pull cards. The two people with the lowest cards would have to talk about themselves to the group. Of course we all knew each other already, but the purpose of the game was so that each person would be forced to see herself for who she really was. We would have to create a new name for ourselves and talk about us as if we were gossiping about a third person. It was a strange exercise that Carmen thought of, but we'd become accustomed to her unusual antics and realized that they usually resulted in something positive so we welcomed the challenge. She called the exercise The B Side.

****

Leah had volunteered to go first.

She began with the first two mandatory sentences, "My name is Lucy. That Leah, she's a trip." Then she continued.

"She's always talking about she needs to leave Walter

and she needs to move on because she knows Walter doesn't want to do right by her but she just sits on her butt and does nothing. Walter is always buying new stuff and spending money he doesn't have like he ain't got no sense. He is selfish and arrogant. He's always claiming to be broke when it comes to helping her. He was a cheater and she still doesn't know if she can trust him. He's always trying to control her..."

Carmen interrupted. "Uh, Ms. what's your name?"

"Lucy."

"Uh, Lucy? We're not trying to hear about Walter. We want to talk about that damn Leah with her slick ass. No male bashing here, Lucy. I know you are new here and don't quite know the rules, but uh..."

We all laughed and Leah/Lucy continued.

"Well, yeah. That's what I'm saying. Leah concentrates on Walter so much she can't even think right. She doesn't really want to be without him, but she knows she will never be happy with him. I don't know if she stays because she's just used to being with him and afraid of being alone. Or if she's caught up in the fact that he's her son's dad. Or if she feels she's invested five years, so she may as well wait it out and hope for the best."

"I think she just wishes he would step up to the plate and be the responsible man he should be. Though she could have almost any man she wants, she keeps going back to Walter. But don't y'all let Leah fool y'all. Leah has had some fun. She has dated the most eligible bachelors around. Men that women dream about. Her list of friends reads like a Who's Who in America. She's a pro at appeasing herself with boy toys. Yet, she can't pull any strings to make Walter act right. She wishes Walter could just be real with her again."

The room was silent. Everyone appeared to be in deep thought as if listening to a teacher or watching a good movie. As far as we knew, Walter was a king. He had fine things and we just assumed that he had helped Leah get back on her feet after she had sold everything to raise money to press her CDs. Why else would she choose Walter over all of the other nice, wealthy men who persisted? Walter must really shower her with love. At least that's what we assumed.

Lucy/Leah continued.

"Leah has been proposed to by a couple of dream men she's dated but whenever anyone gets close to her where she feels she's really getting into them, she finds something wrong with them. Actually, there's something wrong with her crazy ass. Truth is she doesn't know what it is about Walter that keeps her bound. He's told her they will never marry. He says they are fine as they are so why should they mess it up? For years her stupid ass bought into that until she started to think about her getting older and being with a Negro for forty years with no security whatsoever. Just stupid!!! Stupid!!! Stupid!!!!!!! Who ever heard of a fine, successful chick like Leah putting up with that type of mess?!!!"

"Maybe, she's a little too controlling. Her male friends say she's too independent. Her female friends think she's waiting on something that doesn't exist. Who knows? I don't know what the problem is but personally I think she should get what she wants or die trying. Fuck a half-ass man!! But I guess that's what her crazy butt wants to do, huh? With that damn Walter."

Leah paused. She had been talking a while and

wondered if she was beginning to bore the ladies. No one spoke, so Leah continued.

"You know what Leah does? She saves mean messages and letters from him and listens and rereads them whenever she feels herself falling back into Walter. She does that to remind herself of who Walter is. Otherwise, she'd probably question herself as to whether or not sweet, loving Walter really said what she thinks he said."

"She gets really mad at the fact that she can not leave Walter and stay gone. It's like she's a failure. Anything else she wants to do, she gets out there and makes it happen. She pressed her own CDs and sold them through friends, family, beauty shops, etc. to prove to the world that there was an audience that would appreciate her voice and style. She sacrificed and struggled to realize her dreams and yet, she can't truly enjoy it because of that damn Walter. I think she's holding on to who Walter was. He used to buy her things, take her places and make it obvious that he wanted to be with her. All that is gone and yet she stays. Feeling like he takes her for granted. All the while I guess it chips at her ability to be all that she can be. Sometimes she thinks it's just that they've been together for so long that he's just settled now. But maybe it really is just time to move on. Leah is just confused. The worse part about it is she doesn't know when or if the cycle will ever end."

Lucy/Leah paused to wipe the tears from her eyes.

"Outside of that, Leah is one bad mamma-jamma. I know that sounds crazy, but its the truth."

She pluffed the pillow in her chair and sat down.

None of us knew what the response should be. This was

our first time doing this exercise. It wasn't until Carmen began clapping that we knew it was alright or over. Denise then suggested that Carmen go next.

Carmen was clearly moved by Leah's situation. She held her eyes wide and blinked repeatedly, with her eyelids functioning like windshield wipers. She stood up quickly, took a deep breath and began.

"My name is Chocolate Temple. That Carmen, she's a trip. She's just like that damn Leah."

Carmen fell back into her seat and quickly turned to look at Lisa as if to say, 'next.'

That was it. None of us pressed the issue. We all knew that Leah's story was so similar to Carmen's that those three sentences were all that she was able to give at that time.

Lisa stood up.

"Well... my name is Laura. That Lisa, she's a trip..."

Two months later when Chocolate Temple/Carmen actually took a real turn, the conversation ended up somewhere in left field. She did her little introduction and everything and went straight into calling Ms. Carmen out. She cut lose. I don't know where she gets the courage to be so free. I think she's a little crazy. I really do.

"Hi. My name is Chocolate Temple. That Carmen, she's a trip. She thinks she's the shit. Always talking about she can do anything she desires if she puts her mind to it. And she says crazy stuff like, 'God really likes me. He takes special care of me. He hooks me up.' As if she really thinks God is her buddy or something. And she's always talking about Tyrone and blaming

Tyrone for something. Truth is: she's got issues, too."

"She drinks too damn much. She thinks it's okay to get drunk as long as she ain't hitting the pipe or shooting up. But she doesn't realize that it's still an addiction. She says she can't trust Tyrone. Hell, Tyrone can't trust her. She was cursed with this something that just draws men in as if they are hypnotized. I don't know if it is a fortunate or an unfortunate thing for her. Men seem to want her as a trophy. They are mesmerized by her and as a result she usually has surface relationships. Men get all caught up into the fact that they are with Carmen Trenton instead of just Carmen from the South Side of Chicago. I guess that's why she discards them so easily. When she can tell a guy is using her to get attention instead of loving her for who she really is, she loses respect for him and will use him and toss him into the alley of her mind."

"Carmen doesn't want to be considered too different so she downplays everything. She won't share a lot of her successes because she knows people will feel like she's bragging. She made sure she didn't do anything to excel in school because it wasn't cool. She barely studied from seventh grade all the way through college. Her parents were cool with the B's and C's, but Carmen always knew she could have easily gotten A's. But that wouldn't have been the cool thing to do. She worked all through college and since she never thought it made sense to take all of the crazy classes in subjects she would never need in life, she left college in her senior year to work full-time. Just after she passed probation at her job, she was promoted. She was the youngest, the first black and the first woman to hold such a position in her company. She was proud that she had shown society and the racist system at her job that minorities, women, and young people could handle high ranking positions and could do the job better than most, if not all of the members of the 'good ole boys club,' if given a fair chance. She went through so much at that job. For years she plotted to get out of there, but the money was good. Eventually, she felt like the job was too much of a drain on her spirit and she left and started her own business."

"Carmen has been exposed to some of the best life has to offer, including men. Contrary to what everyone else thinks, Carmen feels like the overexposure has stifled her. On one hand she sees in her own family the strong morals and values associated with the simple life of the not so wealthy. She always says if you ain't in touch with regular down home people then you are truly missing out. There is nothing as sweet and pure as fun experienced through a gentle struggle. The key there being gentle. You know what I mean, like everybody tossing in for pizza and a drink or pulling together to pay for the one person who is going through extremely hard times. Those are times that build beautiful memories. But when it's much more than a gentle struggle, and you can't eat at all, there isn't anything pretty about that."

"Then on the other hand she sees the crazy lifestyles and diminished morals and back stabbing that goes on amongst the wealthy. Everyone is worried about what they have, how they can keep it and how they can get more. And because they sometimes have to do whatever it takes to get and keep success, there is no commitment to anything but money. Everything else is up for grabs. Women, children, friends, parents and even their own souls. It can be extremely superficial and empty. But she also sees that money can open closed doors, and enable one to really experience life abroad. So now, Carmen is just all screwed up. She wants the best of both worlds, but in actuality that scenario doesn't exist. And that's where she sits today. On the fence. Afraid to go one-way or the other. Hoping to stay within reach of it all but never really experiencing the totality of anything. She's the same with men. She sits on the fence, never really leaving Tyrone, so its kinda like she's committed, but yet, free to roam. And no matter how much she complains, I think she likes it there. In the middle. On the fence. She just complains to make her morally correct side feel like she desires what society says she should have.

"Yep, that Carmen she's a mess."

"That's an understatement. Carmen's free to roam? You sure Carmen ain't a whore?" Renee asked sarcastically as she struggled to cross her legs.

"Well, I don't think so. What do you think?"

"Well, I guess the answer to that would vary, depending on who was being asked."

"Well, I'm asking you. I mean I thought a whore was someone who sold sex. But let's not take my word for it." Carmen grabbed the dictionary from the nearby bookcase. "Let's see... whore. According to this here American Heritage College Dictionary, whore is a prostitute. A person considered sexually promiscuous. A person considered as having compromised principals for personal gain. That's about what I thought it meant. No, I wouldn't say Carmen is a whore."

Renee sat there with a smirk on her face looking away from the direction where Carmen sat.

"I mean, what do you think Renee? Enlighten me. I mean do you think Carmen fucks to get things from men?"

"No, I didn't say that."

"But you're looking like you have a different opinion. Speak your mind. I dish it and I can take it. Trust me. Don't hold back on my account. See, the difference in me and you is if I thought there was something you should take note of that could possibly help you to be a better person, I'd tell you. You won't. At least you won't tell me, you'd tell everybody else."

"No I wouldn't. If you don't think Carmen is a whore then that's your opinion."

"Yeah, but I just read the definition and you agreed that it didn't apply."

"But you read more than one definition."

"Okay." Carmen read the definition again. "Like I said, none of those apply to Carmen. Well, forget the game. None of that applies to me. I'm not promiscuous."

"You don't think you're promiscuous?"

"Not at all. Let's look up promiscuous. Promiscuous... 'Indiscriminate in the choice of sexual partners. Lacking standards or selection. Casual; random.' That's not me. I am very choosey with who I share my goodies. I don't have casual sex. The men I screw, I'm dating or having regular contact with. So I would still have to say no, I'm not a whore."

"Okay, yeah, but why so many? You don't think that having all those partners is dangerous and that wouldn't constitute being promiscuous?"

"I don't remember a number or maximum in that definition. And what do you mean by 'all those'? Who determines how many is too many? I function under the fingers and toes ordinance. In this lifetime I get to screw as many men as I have fingers and toes. As long as I don't exceed that, then I'm cool."

"But there should be a limit to the number of partners you're willing to have." Renee argued with confidence and conviction..

"And I just told you there is a limit and according to my last count I still have a few slots available. I've been screwing for almost 20 years. You tell me how many partners I'm entitled to. I'll bet I've got some catching up to do."

"Well, I've only had six men in my life."

"Sounds like a personal misfortune if you ask me."

"No, it's because I decided a long time ago that I wasn't going to have just anybody jumping up and down on me."

"I heard that. Neither do I. But let me ask you this, was that by choice."

"Was what by choice?" Renee looked puzzled.

"You having so few partners. Or was it due to lack of options? Because I think I'd rather have twelve fun loving, feel-good relationships than to keep one asshole that mistreats me, just so I can brag about having one partner."

"Well, like they say, whatever floats your boat. That's all that matters."

"That's right, Baby Boo." Carmen said jokingly attempting to ease the tension in the room. "So, what do y'all think? Should there be a limit? And if so, how should it be determined?"

Sharon spoke first. "Well, I'm just wondering how your

crazy butt came up with the fingers and toes thing and how you are able to stick to it. Right about now, I'd need to be an octopus to fit all of mine in." Everyone in the room laughed. Most agreed."And I don't feel bad about it," Sharon added. "That's barely one partner a year. Who can stick to that mess? Who would want to?! Hell, with only six partners, and you aren't married... either you are lying or you've got some hellified toys over there. I can only imagine what would fall out if I opened your closet."

The room filled with laughter. Sharon was talking as if she was joking, but everyone knew Sharon was for real.

"Well, yeah. Some of that goes on. I mean I'd rather do myself than to die with AIDS from a stranger. And to answer your question Sharon, I think ideally you should have one partner and who determines that number? God. It's in the Bible. You all should read it sometimes."

This was a rare time that Renee wished for Rita's presence. Rita would have offered support and she would have had scripture to back her up. Renee could barely remember what the bible said, she definitely couldn't toss out scripture numbers.

"I have one partner... one at a time," Sharon teased.

"Sugar, there is some middle ground in there," Jonay added.

"And other more pleasurable alternatives," said Rudy.

"And what might those be?" Renee asked attempting to trick Rudy into confirming what some already believed about her sexual preference.

Emily interrupted, "Well, there's the tickler. There's the faucet. There's big thick rubber... need I continue?"

"Yes!" Shouted Sharon. "Go on, girl. Go on!"

"You know... cause a girl can't wait on sorry-ass men these days. You'd better know how to help yourself. Then if you should run into a fellow who can add a little icing to the cake... cool." Emily smiled as she slid up to the edge of the couch. "I say to hell with them. Half of them don't know what they're doing anyway."

There were a couple of comments in agreement. "You know that's right. - You can say that again."

That's when Rudy spoke. It seemed like the perfect time for her to speak her peace.

"Who knows better what a woman wants or needs than a woman? With modern technology, anything a man can give you so can a woman. Including a baby. But the difference is, 9 times out of 10, she'll stay to help raise the kid. They say you haven't experienced an orgasm until you've had a woman. That's what they say."

"Well, I damn sho don't believe that!" Veronica replied.

"Me either," added Carmen. "If a woman has the secret, then introduce her to my man, whomever it may be at the time and hopefully she'd be willing to share her knowledge. Because, me, myself, I don't want nothing with titties touching on me. That would be woman, or big, juicy man."

Sharon said, "Well, they say that girl, the big one, the rapper - they say she ain't no joke. If we're looking for teachers, maybe we should send some men to her."

"What's the difference?" Rudy asked. "I've always wondered, if you were in a dark room and someone did you and you didn't know it was a woman until the lights same on, would that make the incident bad? Even if it was the best you've ever felt in your life?"

"Hell yes!" Carmen replied.

"That thought makes me sick," Veronica added. "The whole thing for me is the idea that there's a man with me. That's why I don't get into doing myself. I just don't turn me on like that. There has to be a penis attached. One that has been there since birth, if you know what I mean. Otherwise, the act itself ain't all that great."

"Well you can do yourself and that has nothing to do with you being weird or gay. Masturbation is totally natural. Until you know your own body, you can't guide or help to obtain maximum pleasure." Jonay stated. "No one, male or female is going to know where to go if you don't know or aren't willing to help them find your spot. And in order to find it you're going to have to do some searching. I suggest if you don't know where your pleasure point is, then you go home and explore alone. Usually men want to feel like they are rocking your world and they are not very patient when you are continually saying, that's not it."

"And how do you find it? I'm just curious," Lisa said.

"Well, I have an instructional video at home. I'll bring it so we all can watch it. It's rather interesting. There were a lot of things revealed that I did not know."

"But basically, what are you supposed to do?" Lisa asked.

"You can take these two fingers." Jonay wiggled her pointer and middle finger. "And just gently explore your vagina. Feel around until you notice a spot that is more sensitive than the rest, and that'll be it."

"So, can it be just anywhere? Or is it in the same spot in all women?"

"Well, I think it's in the same general area in all women but I'm not sure. I think I read that somewhere."

"Well, where is the area? Up? Down? Side?" Lisa persisted.

"Up near the top. At least that's where mine is."

"You know what? This group was not supposed to be about turning people into freaks or dikes. We've gotten all off the subject and into the twilight zone somewhere." Veronica snapped.

"You don't think sex and sexuality is relevant to being complete? I beg to differ, Ms Veronica." Amy spoke in her usual educated matter-of-fact manner. "Em, what was it with the faucet? The rest of those things I'm already familiar with."

"Well, girl. You don't know about the faucet? Let me tell you. That is my favorite!" Emily shook quickly as if to shake something off of her. "Girl, when a guy gets to talking crazy, or acting crazy, I just get my Luther CD or some jazz and put it on in the bathroom, I light a few candles to get me a nice mood set and I slide my big butt right underneath that faucet. Honey, honey, honey. Ain't nobody got to come home that night. He ain't got to call. And he ain't missed. When I'm done, I get me a glass of wine, put on a good movie and I'm sleep within a few minutes. Worry-free."

"That's a little too much for me." Veronica said.

"Baby... Don't knock it until you've tried it." Emily smiled.

About two weeks later, Lisa had confided in me that she just couldn't bring herself to rub on her own stuff because she just wasn't that type. But she had tried, the faucet thing.

To use her own words, she said, "Girl, you should have seen me in that kitchen... ass out, ankles up. I hope nobody was walking their dog or nothing. I couldn't get situated quite right in the kitchen sink so I went back to the bathroom. I only tried the kitchen because the bathroom seemed too rough and the flow was too heavy. I thought I'd find a kinder, gentler lover in the kitchen sink but as it turned out, the bathroom was just fine."

I guess my thoughts were written all over my face because she quickly added, "Don't worry Carla, I took the dishes out of the sink first."

But regardless of what she said, I wouldn't be eating or drinking at her spot anymore. Believe that.

A few others apparently found a friend in Mr. Water. All I can say is if it is up to a majority vote amongst The Beautiful Ones, instead of some nasty, sweaty, used strippers, there will be a row of brand new shining, adjustable pressure faucets lined up to entertain us at the bachelorette event.

****

Hard to believe that's Carmen sitting here with that big rock on her hand headed towards marriage. Yep, I surely hope Marcus is marrying Chocolate Temple because he's headed for a hell of a ride if he gets Carmen down off that fence. Mama and Candice like Marcus. They said they had their fingers crossed that he wouldn't hurt her. I'm not really worried about Carmen.

I'm more concerned about Marcus. I know Carmen. I've watched her my whole life and no matter which way she falls, she always lands on her feet.

10

Money Matters

I don't feel guilty. They all keep peeking over at me as if I should feel guilty or something. I still say business before pleasure. If Carmen wants to sit here and act like money isn't important then that's a game she's playing with herself because she ain't fooling me.

Money matters.

Marcus could rub feet, backs, necks, whatever. If he can't rub his hands together and make some dollars appear then he's worthless. I don't care what people think about me. I'm just honest. I can pay to have my feet and anything else rubbed if I so desire. Carmen ain't fooling nobody but herself. If money isn't important to her then why is she always working so hard and pushing herself to do more? It would be cheaper to hire someone to do what Marcus does. At least you don't have to feed and clothe a masseuse. Hell, marrying him is like adopting a child. And they talked about me and said I was crazy. At least Rashaad brought something to the table. He was rich. He was young and he was stupid but that was his own fault. That's what happens when you give a rat caviar. He can't appreciate it. He's from the ghetto. He didn't have a clue as to what to do with eighty million dollars. He was tossing it to every thug and hoodlum in Chicago. Why shouldn't I get my share? And these self-righteous, half-holy ass ladies had the nerve to act as if they felt sorry for him. His ass wasn't innocent. What about the fact that he thought he was using me? Mr. NBA himself. He milks the situation. He uses his celebrity status to get what he wants from everybody. He was sexing every young star struck amateur he could get his hands on. Big money ass! Just teasing those little girls. Showing them what they could possibly get, all the while knowing he wasn't giving up jack. That's why I got him. He thought I was little Ms. ex-football wife. He came to my house and saw the degrees hanging on my wall and thought he was just adding another loop in his belt. I let him walk around all puffed up thinking he was running game on me. All the while, I knew exactly what I was doing. Like I say, people can judge me all they want to. It was like going to a sperm bank, only I picked up a baby and a baby's daddy's checkbook. Like government assistance to the millionth power. People do it all the time to men with "good jobs." But because I was able to do it to one with a "great job," I'm supposed to be a bad person.

Whatever.

My daughter was getting older and we only had about six more years of her child support coming. Her dad's NFL career was coming to an end anyway, and the way he handled his money, who knew if there would be anything left to get? Plus, I had never planned to have only one child. Then came flashy, big-ballin' Rashaad. No condom. No pull out. The opportunity just presented itself. Now, how is that my fault? I know he took those mandatory NBA classes that were designed to prepare him for his new life and, well, basically for me. He was just silly and feeling himself. He was going around bragging about doing me and I didn't hear anyone complain. So, I did him.

So what that I was thirty-six and he was twenty-one. He was legal and so are his child support payments. I don't understand what the big deal was. He doesn't even miss that money. I was surprised I only got four thousand a month. That ain't twenty percent. I damn near get that from Shawna's dad and he doesn't make nearly what Rashaad makes. But I won't complain.

Truth is, I thought I was just about out of the active market. I had experimented with a few sugar daddies and was trying to get myself educated in that arena. I must admit, Rashaad was a gift. He was ignorant, rude and down right nefarious, so I don't feel any guilt behind that one. We used each other. He wasn't trying to settle down with me. He was getting what he wanted and I got what I wanted. Plus, I exposed him to people, places, and things that he would have never known if it wasn't for me. So as payment for that and other services rendered, I'll be able to continue to live like I've become accustomed to living. At least for eighteen more years.

Hell, I love my children just like every other parent does. So I don't care how they judge me. They need not worry about Amy. I'm happy, just as happy as any of them. In the end we'll pull score cards and see who comes out on top. She who lets the broke ass men pull her down or she who lets the ignorant ass men move her up? Carmen is going to have to live with Marcus' brokeness everyday. I'll only see Rashaad in the summer when he picks up Jacob. And yes, I do think about the future. Why do you think I keep myself in somebody's exercise class or boot camp? All that I can't work off, I'll cut off. As long as I keep myself looking good, riding slick and hanging with the right people in the right places, I'll keep me a man with money. It's only the poor and downtrodden who place this big emphasis on how many men you've been with and stuff like that. In my world the bigger the name you tag, the more desirable you become.

Eventually, I'll run across one I really like. Until then, Rashaad's money affords me the opportunity to take my sweet time.

These ladies seem to think romance is a joke. Something to be played with. That's why they keep losing. Romance is a business. It is to be treated as such. Complete with preparations, plans and negotiations. I hope Carmen is doing this whole thing as a front for a bigger plan. Hopefully, she's still fooling around with Ace. Ace is getting a million dollars a book, I hear. He and Carmen claim to be best friends. I hope she isn't that stupid. Who needs a friend like that? She needs to make that work for her. I don't care if he's married or not. If she knew like I know, she'd cuff him and a couple of others. What could he say about it? That's the best thing about those married ones. They can't give you too much drama. It's funny, they do seem to be the most possessive ones. But there's still only so much attention and time they can devote to crawling up your ass lest wifey may suspect something.

Thank goodness for wifey. She absorbs most of the stress and drama. She gets most of the money too, but as long as I get my fair share I'm okay with it. I hope Carmen's working some type of merger like that.

Otherwise, this cannot be real. If she really loves this Marcus guy then why not just be with him? She doesn't have to do anything crazy like marry him. She must know something none of us knows. Maybe he has a large settlement coming from a lawsuit or something. That has to be it because he isn't even all that cute. The truth will eventually come out. It always does.

****

Amy looked over her shoulder into the waiters face as he refilled her water. "Can you bring the check as soon as you get a chance?"

"Sure. I'll bring it right out. I put everything on one bill. Is that okay?"

"I guess so. I'll take care of this one." Amy looked towards Carmen. "If you're willing to take on that, I guess I can take care of this." Amy waved her hand cross the table, then quickly changed the subject.

"Now I know we've been here too long. The flame has burned out on this candle." She picked up the candle holder and surveyed it's sloppy remains. "That's life, huh? Nothing stays new and fresh for long."

11

Hallelujah !!

"Praise God! Oh hallelujah, Lord!" Rita closed her eyes and held her open palms towards the ceiling. "Ummmmm," she moaned. "God is surely good. Thank you, Lord. Thank you."

Rita's eyes were still closed when she bowed her head and embraced herself as she rocked slightly back and forth. She began to mumble something. No one could make out what she was saying and no one really tried. This was classic Rita. Every since she'd found religion she'd been prone to behave like this. Some still questioned her sincerity. After all, she did happen to find religion after she'd married the biggest baller in town.

****

Wild Bill is what they call him. Bill was involved in a little bit of everything. Enough of everything to afford that, fancy home and the Land Cruiser and the Benz and the jewelry and the custom clothing. There was a two-lane bowling alley in their basement, a game room bigger than *Gaming On You*, the best game room in the city, an indoor pool in the basement and their own private theater complete with reclining seats. Yeah, Bill was ballin'.

He had so much money that he decided he wouldn't inconvenience himself by moving all the way out to the suburbs. No, Bill found a huge, old church right in the heart of Hyde Park. He put an eight foot wrought iron fence around it, some surveillance cameras, and he built a live-in guard shack and called it a day. He didn't like the look of the church so he totally remodeled it. He had all the rich cherry wood trim painted black, he got stark white carpet throughout the top two floors and put money green carpet in the basement. Bill was a character. But not any more, according to Rita.

Supposedly, those church spirits grabbed a hold of them both one night. She says it was the scariest thing she'd ever experienced. She claims God spoke to her and Wild Bill – separately of course. God led her to scripture, I Corinthians 7:39. She said she was just about to leave wild Bill because she felt guilty when she saw what his drugs were doing to people. She felt bad driving past the corner liquor store where ex doctors, lawyers, mailmen, janitors, teachers and students spent days and nights begging for pennies to finance their habits and her luxuries. She no longer could visit old friends knowing the family hardships inflicted by their fathers, mothers, sons and daughters were direct results of her need to feed on greed. She found herself in a lonely place.

Then one night while she was in her vintage tub with the gold paw feet, laid back relaxing, smoking a joint, she heard a creaking sound. Even though she was listening to her favorite mellow me out tune, she could still hear the creaking. Bill wasn't home and they didn't have any kids. She peeked over at the security monitor and could see that the guard was up and alert and nothing seemed out of place or conspicuous, but nevertheless the creaking persisted.

For a moment she thought maybe the weed was bad or something. Maybe it had her mind playing tricks on her. But she remembered smoking a joint from the same bag when she woke up that morning. Nothing crazy happened then. No, it wasn't the weed. It couldn't be.

That's when she realized it had to be one of three things, God, the devil or Mrs. Abernathy, the woman she'd stole her first pack of squares from when she was eleven years old. Yeah, a lot of time had passed and Mrs. Abernathy had been dead for at least ten years, but Rita dared not underestimate the power of Mrs. Abernathy. Mrs. Abernathy could hold a grudge forever.

Rather than face Mrs. Abernathy or God or the devil himself, Rita had jumped out of the tub and sprinted out the door with nothing but the robe she'd managed to grab. She jumped into her car and drove around for a while until she finally decided to go to her mother's house. Her mother was, as she still is, very poor. She lives on the low end in the heart of the ghetto. Rita went down there and didn't even think once about whether it was safe to go up in that building with nothing on but her robe. She was like a bull headed towards the red cloth. Nobody dared bother her. After listening to her mother go on and on about how Rita needed to ask for forgiveness and clean her life up and serve the Lord, her mother gave her a small bottle of liquid. She told Rita it was blessed oil. She told her to go home and put a little around her house. She didn't need much, just a little. She should even put some on the door before she entered. Her mother told her the oil would ward off the demons and protect her as long as she would promise to clean up her life.

Rita did as she was told and she ain't seen or heard a demon since. She hasn't smoked weed either. That was one of the promises she'd made the night she got the blessed oil. Anyway, after that, Rita was really going to leave Bill when one day she dropped her Bible and when it fell on the floor it was opened to I Corinthians 7, and her eyes went straight to verse 39. That was a sign that she had to stay.

Some street folks tell a whole different story. They say Wild Bill was trapped. He'd gotten so big that he had no peace. The police were after him. There were young guys who worked for him, that were feeling like they deserved to be him. Others thought they were him. New hustlers were scheming. They instantly wanted all Wild Bill had accumulated over twenty years. Women couldn't be trusted, one young girl even tried to set him up to be killed. The streets say the walls were closing in on wild Bill and he had no place to go but to church. Bill had money put up and contrary to his past immature thinking, he realized he actually cared whether he lived or died. It didn't take much for Rita to convince him to "give his life to the Lord."

I myself didn't believe their whole lil' change and I still don't know if I believe it. It was all too convenient. Plus, all that commotion she started up in the church – I just don't believe a supposedly saved, sanctified and filled with the Holy Ghost Christian would have initiated that kind of mess. Carmen was a member of that church for ten years before they asked her to teach that class. Rita wasn't there good three years and she goes and writes an anonymous letter to the pastor, talking about she didn't feel Carmen was the type of woman that should be teaching young girls. The letter talked about Carmen being single, having lots of male friends and her being of poor character. She called her a back-slider and all that sort of stuff, too. When Pastor questioned Carmen about the *Better Safe Than Sorry Health Day* she'd set up, she knew the information had to have come from Rita. Rita was the only person Carmen had consulted regarding that day. She was planning to take her entire class of young ladies to the local Board of Health where they were to be tested for AIDS and other venereal diseases, given birth control, hear lectures, and watch a short film about safe sex. She was a little uneasy about the whole thing because the girls had voted to keep it secret. She'd asked Rita what she thought and Rita had quoted the Bible as she always seemed compelled to do since she got saved – 'Proverbs 1:7-1:16' Rita had said with her eyebrows raised so high they almost blended with the hair on top of her head.

Carmen really respects Rita's dedication to the word. She is one of the few that is foolish enough to buy into Rita's Holy drama act. Carmen says she equates Rita's passion for things Holy with the passion of a blind man who experiences virgin vision at the ripened age of sixty… The man with the new vision will try to see everything he can as soon as he can. He is so passionate about his new vision that he almost pushes himself to the point of detriment. Who can blame him?

He has to pack sixty years of visual experiences into whatever time he has left in his life. Carmen believes Rita lived foul for so long that she's simply trying to make up for lost time – balance out her life – kiss up to God / brown nose if you will. She wants to be sure God knows she appreciates His acceptance of her, after all she's done wrong. The ultimate display of appreciation is to use the gift, Carmen says. Rita is just trying to use the gift. But all that talk is stuff Carmen says. I've never heard Rita say anything of the sort.

After talking to Rita, Carmen tossed and turned all night. Her approach was new and different and she wanted to be sure she'd considered all angles of possible repercussions. The next morning she got up bright and early and took those girls to the planned health fair.

Rita told it all.

Carmen never even confronted her. She didn't say a word about it. She told me she felt she'd done the right thing.

I think she should have said something. Now, because of Rita, Carmen no longer teaches the class. She loved teaching that class.

****

"Just look at Rita sitting over there with her eyes closed, mumbling, trying her best to squeeze out a tear or two. I'm glad they didn't ask me to be in their little club. I couldn't stomach these phony people on a regular basis. I hope this waiter hurries and brings this check. I don't want to be the first person to leave but I am soooo ready to go."

Candice, Carmen's youngest sister stuffed her arms into her coat then rambled through her purse searching for her car keys.

Carla replied, "If it's getting to you that bad then you need to go ahead and leave. I'll call you tonight once I get mama on the line and fill both of you in on the rest of the details. Here comes the waiter anyway."

"Now that Carmen's getting married, I wanna see if Ms. Holy writes a praise letter to pastor taking back all that stuff she said. Sitting over there crying. She's probably crying because she feels like an idiot. Look at her." Candice stood up, picked up her purse and prepared to leave. She couldn't help but frown as she watched Rita's every move.

"Oh... Praise Him, praise Him," Rita said between sniffles. "Hallelujah!!"

12

Time Will Tell

Dear Diary,

Today was a difficult day. The evening was longer than I expected. The silence was more intense than I imagined. It feels good to be home. Alone.

Carmen's pen skipped strokes as she continued writing.

I'm so glad it's out in the open now. By tomorrow, the whole city will know. Better yet, the whole USA. It feels good to have a partner... to know who my date will be... and most importantly it feels good to have a reason to say no.

For so long I've felt like I had to say yes... to leave doors open and explore the possibilities. It gets old. Now that I have Marcus, I often wonder how many options I really had. Life is so weird. You spend all your time trying to figure out the answer, yet, there isn't one answer that fits. At least I don't think so.

"Do I love him?"

I think it's all in your mind. I think you make yourself love certain people. I would never tell Marcus that, but my friend Mr. Time is going to keep showing up and ultimately, time will tell. Time will tell that we're not really governed by a magic love angel. I believe you choose the person that fits into your life and your lifestyle as smoothly as possible and go from there.

Spring frequently asked, "What's love got to do with it?"

When the haze clears, Marcus will have to choose to be with me and like everyone else, we'll have to dig in and work hard to keep our love flowing. I used to believe in soul mates. I used to believe in true love. I've loved some good men. They may not have fit into my life as I changed or redirected my efforts but they were still good men. Some crazy, some lazy, but still good for somebody. I used to believe love alone was enough. Now I believe even love needs a companion. Love isn't large enough alone. It needs fillers in order to fit. Fillers like tennis, golf, books, music, dinners and dancing, poetry, flowers, tears of joy and pain, lawnmowers, bubble baths, scrabble, walks and long talks, movies, art, basketball and football games, front porches, backyards and tall glasses of iced tea...

Right now, Marcus fits. He takes care of me. Imagine... It's like he saw me when I was lost and running butt naked through a jungle. He didn't have shit. He was naked himself. But he took the time out to pick a fig leaf, a big fig leaf, and he clothed me.

Then he offered me shelter in his raggedy hole-filled, smelly tent. It wasn't what I was used to, or what I desired, but it was his best. Well, in that scenario, when I get back to the city (my senses) where I'm from, I can't just leave him naked, nor can I forget that he covered me when I needed covering.

So what do I do? I marry him. For all it's worth, I owe him. So that's what I do, I marry Marcus.

Carmen closed the notepad and her eyes as she drifted off

to sleep.

Part Three

Countdown

13

Lean on Me

Jonay stood in her living room almost perfectly centered in the corner of the floor to ceiling windows which exposed the perfect midnight blue backdrop for Chicago's skyline. She had chosen this floor, the thirty-fourth floor, because thirty-four was how old she was when she was finally able to fulfill her dream of living here, in this building in downtown Chicago on the prestigious Lake Shore Drive. She paced side to side taking only tiny steps due to the lack of available space.

"Does everyone know why we're here today? We called this special meeting for a couple of reasons. First of all we didn't want Carmen to be in attendance... She is away in Atlanta right now working on one of her client's homes and we thought this would be the perfect opportunity to discuss a few things without her trying to interrupt or run things. We all know that it was Carmen who came up with this whole support group concept. She did that out of love for us and what she saw as an apparent need for us to help educate and build one another up. This group has really been a blessing. We've seen major changes effected since its inception."

"Well, you all remember the criteria for membership was that you had to be a good friend to at least two other members prior to being accepted and you had to be single. When Carmen announced that she was getting married, I don't think any of us thought about what that really meant. That means Carmen will no longer be with us. I personally can't imagine The Beautiful Ones without Carmen. A few of us have discussed changing the *single rule*, but I know Carmen would not agree with that. She has always felt that single women have a negative influence on married women in these type of discussion groups.. Especially when they meet on a regular basis. So, I just wanted to put that out there for feedback or comments."

"Also, we've only got four weeks until the big day. We need to plan this bachleorette event. Someone suggested we use Ace's house. Sharon asked him and he wasn't too cool with it but he said he'd let her know."

"Wasn't too cool with it? Why?" Veronica asked.

"Well, he isn't cool with the whole idea of her getting married."

"Ain't that a trip? He's married. Why doesn't he want her to be married?" Emily asked.

Sharon answered. "Well, that's Ace. You know how he is about his Carmen. He probably feels like their friendship is being threatened or something. He'll be okay."

"Girl, ain't nobody thinking about his ass. He'd better get over it." Emily stated with much attitude.

"So how many strippers are we gonna have? I say at least four. There are a lot of us." Renee said.

"You all know Carmen doesn't like strippers. I say we do something different, something Carmen will enjoy and remember." Rudy spoke with confidence.

"Forget what Carmen likes. What about what we like?" Renee joked half-heartedly.

"I say we have a big party with all of her close associates, male and female. We can have some poets perform special pieces for her... you know Carmen loves poetry... and Leah can sing a little something... and things of that sort. You know what I mean? An earthy type of setting."

Rudy hoped the ladies would agree with her. She definitely did not want to have to sit through a show of naked men flaunting tools they couldn't even use.

Lisa agreed.

"That sounds like something Carmen would love." She said.

"Does everybody agree with that?" Rudy asked.

All the ladies agreed.

"Then there we have it. I guess we should give all suggestions to you, Sharon? Or Carla?"

"Yeah, that would be cool." Sharon spoke for she and Carla since Carla had to work and could not make it to the meeting.

Jonay began speaking again.

"Also, there's another issue. It has been brought to my attention that Carmen is in a bad way, I guess you could say. Her financial situation is totally screwed up. She put all of her money into having art reproductions done and as we all know, the printing company went out of business with her money. All of her money. She has been struggling and trying to make ends meet, but unfortunately it looks like she's going to lose her house."

"What?! You lying." Emily sounded like Mrs. Whittaker, the lady from 69th street who watched and reported on everyone in the neighborhood where Carmen and Emily grew up. Mrs. Whittaker was first to report on Mr. Frison's, Emily's dad's, affair with Mr. Holter, Emily's mom's best friend's husband and next door neighbor.

"What about Marcus?" Asked Leah.

"What about him?" Amy added. "He can't do anything but try to rub away the heart attack all of this mess is going to give her."

"Well, I didn't reveal that so that we could gossip about her or judge her. It was suggested earlier by one of our members that we give Carmen our bank. We were saving it to invest in something, why not Carmen? We've been saving since the night the guy came to our meeting and spoke with us about finances. When was that, February? We should have almost ten thousand dollars by now. It was suggested that we give it to her as a wedding gift."

"You mean to she and Marcus?" Renee snarled.

"However you want to think of it. I think of it as helping her, but, that will be her husband so ..." Jonay turned the palms of her hands up towards the fancy contemporary chandelier that hung above her.

"Well, I don't understand why we're going to give money to help someone who has a man. She's one step ahead of us. At least she has help." Renee contested.

"What help? You know Marcus ain't got a pot to piss in." Amy barked.

"Well, that's her choice. So now my money has to go to

support her and her man? Hell, I've got bills too. Maybe we could split the money between mine and Carmen's bills." Renee titled her head at an angle like a confused dog or cat would.

"I'm barely standing myself and I'm supposed to let a grown woman and her man lean on me?" Renee crossed her arms and was clearly irritated.

"Why would we not give it to her just because she has a man. Is that supposed to be her punishment? If we would have given it to her otherwise, I don't understand why it should be different now. We all know that she would give it to us and probably will when she gets everything back in order."

"Probably," Renee snarled. "That's a big word."

"Well, we're not suggesting it be a loan. Carmen is the reason for this whole thing even being. And it isn't like she's a regular screw up. That misfortune was beyond her control."

Jonay strained with the release of each word as she pleaded Carmen's case.

"I sympathize with that, but I've got credit cards that are maxed out and other things that I could think of to spend my money on. It *is* my money too," Renee argued.

Sharon broke in.

"Listen, you know what? Then why don't you take whatever you've put in! And anybody else who isn't willing to have their money go towards helping Carmen save her house can get theirs too! Why don't we just do it that way? Get your pennies because you are right, they are your pennies. Then those willing can give theirs to this girl and save her house. Cause all this talking is bullshit! Just bullshit. I can't even believe we're debating this."

"I'm not saying I'm totally against it. But you've got to tell me something more than what's been said. What makes Carmen any different that the rest of us that I should give my money to fund her bad decisions?" Renee persisted.

"You know what, Renee? I done said take your money. Evidently you need it worse that we do."

"I mean she's running around here paying for weddings and shit... She can't be too broke." Renee snapped.

Sharon stopped as she reached for her planner, which she had placed on the glass coffee table at the start of the meeting. She blinked her eyes slowly as she turned to look at Renee.

"What two voted you in this motherfucker? I've been wondering that for a while." With that she grabbed the planner and headed towards the door.

"Y'all let me know the outcome of this stupid shit. I'm gone."

The heavy door closed with a solid thump. It was almost as perfect an exit as if Sharon would have slammed it.

The room was silent, except for Renee's incessant chatter about how she just wanted to know why she should have to support someone else's drama. Within minutes, almost as if on cue, everyone stood and offered excuses for having to leave. Not one person requested their money be returned. Not even Renee. After hours of being irritated at the sound of Renee's voice, Jonay had finally asked Renee to leave. She told her it was way past her bedtime and she had to work on a report and do some reading for work before she turned in. None of that was true.

On her way out the door Renee had commanded, "Oh, you can leave the money in there. I'm just gonna see if they do the same when my shit gets raggedy."

The door closed behind Renee with a loud thump, as it had closed behind each and every other invited guest that evening. The pressurized pump at the top wasn't aware of the group's discourse, which resulted in Jonay's displeasure with her final guest and therefore, it breathed a routine unbiased breath into its mechanism despite Jonay's efforts to slam it extra hard.

14

Soul Music

I can't sleep. This bed is too damn cushy. I'm not used to all this fancy stuff. My butt just can't adjust to this twelve hundred dollar comforter. I think I went overboard when I bought this. For twelve hundred dollars seems like it should rub me and sing lullabies. But it's so beautiful. I just couldn't pass it up. The moment I saw it in that specialty boutique in Buckhead, I knew it was perfect for Boston's bed. He's gonna love this. It blends perfectly in this room. I must say, I am good. But of course Boston knows that. That's why I'm here. Matter of fact, Boston knows how good I am. On several levels.

I wish I hadn't had to come here, but Boston prepaid me a couple of months ago and I had to use most of his money to pay my delinquent bills. If I could've come up with the money somehow, I would have preferred to just give him a refund and be done with it. I don't need the temptation. I can't be playing with fire. That's why I've been busting my ass trying to finish this place before Friday. If only the stores hadn't been so crowded yesterday, I'd be done. I really, really don't want to be here when he returns from his road trip on Friday. That's why I picked this week to come and finish picking out art and accents for his place. I checked the schedule carefully and this was the perfect opportunity to get in and out of here. I've got one more day to get this done and get safely home to my fiancé, Marcus. It still sounds awkward when I say that.

****

"This is nice, Boston. What a great design! This is tight!" I stood in the center of the dramatic, marble tiled foyer of the newly built home. "You come here so often you needed to buy something. But my goodness Boston, about five families could live in here."

"Well, I figured you might need a place for you and the kids to go when your husband-to-be starts stressing you out."

"So you're offering this mini-mansion as my secret place? Now, if that's the case then I need to see a big neon sign out front that says, 'No hoochies, smoochies or coochies except that of Ms. Carmen Trenton'," I said jokingly. "You've got to let me decorate this joint, B."

"Who else would decorate your house?" Boston emphasized "your" as he held the keys out towards me.

"Oh, that's cute Boston. But I won't be visiting you after I'm married. I keep telling you, you've got me pegged wrong."

"Well, this Christmas I thought I'd give you a present you'd always remember me by."

"You're so cute Boston."

"I spend half a million dollars on a woman who's marrying someone else and all I can get is 'cute'?" Boston grabbed my hand and led me through the would be dining area into the bright, beautiful kitchen. There in the kitchen was a big red bow suspended across the room by a thin white string. I turned back to look at Boston and his 6'6" perfectly chiseled body seemed to float in its own special glow, like a full-body form fitted halo. He was smiling proudly as he pointed to my name on the papers on the counter.

OWNER: Carmen Trenton

"What?!" I whispered. I felt myself getting weak. Boston must have sensed it, too. In one quick, smooth motion he swooped me up into his arms.

"I love you, Carmen. I know I've been unwilling to commit in the past, but I'm ready. I want to spend the rest of my life with you. There is no other woman in the world for me."

I placed both my hands on his face and kissed him gently. On his lips, his cheek, his nose, his eyes, then his neck and chest. Boston leaned back against the counter near the sink as I shifted my body and wrapped my legs around his waist resting the weight of my legs on the counter behind him. Boston's hands spread wide in cupping position across the two firm masses which in any normal position would have been well cushioned ass cheeks. His body tilted out and seemed to scoop perfectly beneath his full hands which struggled to handle all of me and my full bottom. His awakened manhood pressed firmly against the back of his hands, the center of my butt, and anything it could reach. Boston always had a healthy libido. That was the main reason we kept in contact these past couple of years.

Boston grabbed my loose-fitting, tye-dyed dress which was already lifted well above my waist and pulled it over my head tossing it to the floor. Then he grabbed the string on my hip and like a tiger attacking his prey, he ripped the thong and tore it away from my body.

In response, my sucking of his top lip changed to a slight bite. I held his lip between my teeth as I sat still allowing the warm rush of passion to overtake my body.

Boston lifted my body and turned to sit me on the counter. I held my legs lifted above the counter in butterfly position allowing Boston full sight of my appreciation. Boston leaned towards me as he worked with the buckle of his pants. He kissed my nipples... then a wild, sloppy, wet beastly lick as he took a step forward to present me with his other gift which was now exposed and flirting with my appreciation. Just as our body parts concluded their formal hello's, and prepared to get deep into conversation, I heard a voice. I realized we had not shut the door behind us when we entered the house.

"Wait, wait, Boston. Did you hear that?"

Boston continued kissing and licking as he attempted to give me that second portion of his gift. I wiggled and backed away from within reach of his manhood which was standing strong bobbing around enthusiastically like a kid anticipating candy.

"No, wait Boston," I whispered as the voice came closer.

"Carmen... Carmen," the voice called.

Who was it? And how did he know my name?

"Carmen."

I pushed my hands against Boston's chest and pleaded with him to wait.

"Carmen." The voice sounded familiar now.

Boston grabbed a handful of my hair at the back of my head forcing my head to tilt back as he gnawed at my neck. The voice kept coming.

"Carmen. Carmen."

I couldn't see a face. My eyes rolled somewhere in the back of my head as Boston stroked my appreciation and my will to resist weakened.

"Carmen," the voice called again as the hand belonging to the body with the familiar voice pressed my shoulder.

"Carmen. Wake up. Are you okay? Carmen. You okay, baby?"

I opened my eyes and there stood Boston. Fine as he could be. Bare-chested with the pair of zebra-print, easy access front-slit pajama pants I'd bought for him last Christmas. He looked like deep chocolate. I had flashes of him, the microwave, and something warm, all over my body. I struggled to snap back into reality. With squinted eyes I looked at him, took a deep breath and stretched to steal a few more moments.

"Oh... Hey, Boston."

I paused wondering just how much of my dream he had experienced.

"What are you doing here? What day is it?"

He smiled. "What day is it? It's Thursday. That must have been some good sleep. Were you having a nightmare or something?"

"No. No. Not at all," I said as I rubbed my hands across my face.

"You sure?" he asked as he leaned down and pulled me up to hug me. I breathed deeply. As he hugged me, I noticed a spatula in one of his hands, and I could instantly smell Boston's magic.

"What do you have going on in there?"

"Oh... a little bacon, a little French toast..." Boston teased. He knew what I was waiting to hear. "Oh, yeah, and some potatoes." He smiled.

"What?! Oh, my God. Let me get myself prepared for this." Boston cooked the best potatoes in the world. I could eat those potatoes everyday of the week.

"I ran you some bath water," he said as he walked out of the room.

"Thanks, Boston. You are just too much for me." I spoke in a syrup-sweet way.

Boston always made me that way. He was too good to be true... At least, when you could catch him.

As I slipped off my oversized t-shirt that I had taken from one of his dresser drawers, Boston spoke loudly from down the hall.

"Brace yourself. Cause you ain't ready for these new treasures." He was referring to music. Boston and I loved dusties and had our own private little dusty appreciation club.

We would call each other and share old hits we'd find at various music stores hidden in the bellies of our old neighborhoods. "I've got this new hook up."

"Where?"

"You don't need to know all of that. Just relax and get ready for heaven." He started the marathon off with one of our favorite groups, The O'Jays, *Stairway to Heaven*. Then, Stevie Wonder's , *Blame It On The Sun*, Bobby Womack's, *That's the Way I Feel About Cha*, Phyllis Hyman's, *Betcha By Golly Wow*, Barry White's, *I've Got So Much To Give*, Blue Magic's, *What's Come Over Me*, Marvin Gaye's, *You're All I Need To Get By*, so on and so on...

    I sat there amongst what must have been a dozen lit candles, in an oversized Jacuzzi flooded with thick bubbles, listening to my favorite music, anticipating my favorite food prepared by my sometimes favorite man and wished for time to stop here. At least for ten to fifteen years.

****

    After what seemed like an hour of paradise, I relaxed back against the tub contemplating as to whether or not I should have a quick visit with Mr. water. I could tell I was going to need some help resisting thoughts of Boston.

    "These potatoes are getting cold!" He yelled from the kitchen.

    "I'm on my way," I replied.

    I walked into the kitchen wearing an exercise bra, a thong and a towel around my waist. I wasn't looking for trouble, I just didn't want to wrinkle my skirt. Boston prepared my plate and sat it on the table in front of me between my sterling silver fork, knife and spoon. He had already neatly arranged the syrup, ketchup, jelly (grape and apple), tall glass of milk, glass of ice water and a cup with a Lipton tea bag in it on the table. As I placed the linen napkin in my lap, Boston poured hot water from the teapot into my fine china. That was one of the items I'd purchased the other day.

    "How beautiful," I thought to myself. "Boston, you are a King. I just adore you."

    "It's nothing. You know I don't mind. By the way, did I

tell you how fine you're looking today Miss?"

"No Sir, but thank you. You're looking like Sunday Morning yourself."

Boston smiled. He knew that was the finest compliment he could receive from me. Sunday Morning was my favorite time of all.

"So how do you like your pieces?"

"Looks good."

"How about the oil painting in the front hallway? That's called, *Take Me To The Water*. It's by Ulysses Jacobs."

"I like it."

"The stone statue in the living room is by an artist by the name of Bryn Mteke. It's from Zimbabwe," I said between bites. "It's made of springstone which is just another name for black serpentine. It's a stone that sculptors in Zimbabwe use a lot. You can usually tell by it's smooth sort of greasy feel. I love it. That and verdite are my favorite stones for sculptures. Verdite is that stone that's a kind of an emerald green color or sometimes it's brownish..."

"It looks good, too. Everything looks good. Real good." Boston smiled a half smile that made me nervous.

"I'm glad you like it. You've got some great pieces and I was able to get you great deals. I wish I could have kept a few of these pieces for myself."

"You know you are welcome to visit them anytime you wish."

"I'll remember that. What are you doing here today? I thought you all weren't coming back until after the game Friday night."

"I couldn't rest knowing you were here and this would probably be my last chance to see you as Carmen Trenton. My Carmen Trenton. So I hopped the first plane out this morning and came to see my Carmen."

"You'd better get back. Won't you be fined for that?"

"It's just money. This is more important. As long as I'm in Orlando tomorrow by shoot around, it should be cool."

"Well, it's good seeing you. I've missed you. But unfortunately I'm going to have to get out of here and get the rest of this shopping done. I've got quite a few things that I still have to get."

"That's cool. I'll just go with you if that's okay."

"Sure. I could use some company." I was pleasantly surprised at the thought of spending the day with Boston. Boston was a very busy man, or so he made it seem. He never had much time for frolicking in public. In fact, not once in the history of our dating had we spent an entire afternoon out. All of our time had been private time.

Boston and I spent the day shopping, joking and enjoying each other's company. On our way back to his place we stopped at the market and Boston got some fresh vegetables and other ingredients needed to prepare a meal for a Queen. Boston was laying it on me. He was saying all the right things. Doing all the right things. He made me feel special. This was typical Boston. That's how I nicknamed him The King. He was royalty and he made me feel like his Queen. Boston was my dream man. He was cool and classy yet tough and somewhat thuggish. He had an earthy aura about himself. He was confident and courageous. His style was his own. Unique. People were afraid of Boston.

Boston didn't buy what we used to call, "wolf tickets." Once you challenged him you'd better be able to back that shit up. He would beat your ass! It's like ass-whipping was a sport to him. Boston Stone didn't take no mess. I felt so safe and secure with him. He was what we refer to as a man's man. That's what I loved about him. And that's what I hated about him. Nobody ruled Boston. He did what he wanted to do. He showered me with affection because he wanted to... when he wanted to. He doesn't function on command. He would come into my life, wooo me and make me feel like my life was meant to be with him. Then, everytime I'd unlock the gate to my heart and prepare to invite him in, I'd discover he was gone. He was like a magician who'd mastered these horrible disappearing acts and I hated him for it. Only because I think I loved him, only deep inside I knew I couldn't have him. He was a floater. If I could just learn to ride the waves. But screw that. I'm Carmen Trenton. I had to continually remind Boston of that.

"I'm not your part-time whore, Boston," I'd say. "You can't just come to town and expect me to be ready and waiting. You have to call me more than once every two weeks, send flowers, take me somewhere, send me a plane ticket or something. Surprise me. I don't know what you're used to but you'd better ask somebody about Carmen Trenton."

I'd given this and similar speeches to Boston at least every other month since I'd known him. But Boston was a different breed. He wasn't impressed or the least bit affected. Like clockwork, after a couple of weeks he'd call with his usual free spirited, "What's up, Miss?" I'd spend the first couple of minutes chastising him in my own way, and the rest of the time searching my soul for the key to my heart with hopes of catching him before he'd disappear again.

Now here we are, him sitting on the floor resting his body between my legs as I lean back snugly into the corner of his suede L-shaped sofa... his strong arms resting on the top of either thigh.

"Boston, you've got to hold that oil up some," I instructed as I separated his thick, black twist.

I gently applied the oil to his brown scalp, then massaged it as seductively as I could. This wasn't an ordinary scalp oiling. It was nothing like what I'd do for my son or my daughter after washing their hair. No, this treatment was reserved for Boston.

I wonder if Boston, Tyrone or even Ace are really the problem. Maybe it's me. I thought to myself. Here I am in a position women would die to be in and for some reason I won't compromise. This big, black, fine ass King rubbing on me. He'd better stop now before I have those muscles stretched out cross-corners, tied to that damn bed in there. Umph, umph, umph! Lord give me strength. This isn't worth it Carmen. Boston just wants to visit. Marcus is willing to stay.

"I'm done, Boston," I said as I screwed the top on the jar of oil. Boston leaned his head back against my chest.

"Wait, sit up. You're gonna get oil on the shirt."

"It's okay. It's my shirt."

"You're right." I held his head to my chest as if he were an infant as I stroked his hairline with my fingers. His eyes were closed. He spoke in a low tone.

"You know you're a very special person, Carmen."

"So are you, Boston."

"No, I mean it. I hope that guy realizes what he's getting in you. You know, I always assumed in the end it would be you and me cruising the world in a Winnebago. Tossing tents, being each other's only concern. Potatoes cooking over a campfire. O'Jays, Heatwave and Blue Magic blowing with the wind. Humph. I guess I was wrong."

Now my eyes were closed. It felt good to hear that Boston had dreamed my same dreams. That he did realize that our relationship was something special. I lay there thinking about life and wondering if this was a sign from God or a test from the devil, when all of a sudden Boston and his backup singers began to serenade me. *"Let me hold you tight, if only for one night..."* Luther seemed to be putting his best vocals forward to help Boston communicate his feelings. Boston lay there with his heart wide open, singing soul songs. I could feel myself falling. I prayed a silent prayer thanking God for the warmth of love and asking for His mercy. This was getting to be more than I could bear. I questioned any negative thought I'd ever had about Boston. Come on, Lord, talk to me, I silently pleaded. I don't know if my direct line had a bad connection or what, but next thing I knew, I was getting messages through the music.

"Ooohhh, ooohhhh..." the Temptations, *Just My Imagination* was two-stepping its way through the speakers. I let out a deep sigh. Next up was Dorothy Moore's, *Misty Blue*.

That song there, was all too close to our reality. I found myself slipping into sadness.

Finally, Al Hudson's, *Can't keep Running Away* followed by Miki Howard's, *Love Under New Management* had me damn near in tears. This had to be more than a coincidence. I felt drained. The battle between good and evil was too much for me. I reached down, placed my hand on top of Boston's and held it still to stop his caressing of my thigh. Then I kissed his forehead, draped my arm over his shoulder and rested the palm of my hand on his chest. We laid there motionless, on his couch, barely daring to breathe. I figured I'd meet him in that kitchen, in my dream where I left him.

The next morning I woke to the sounds of Al Hudson's, Guess You Didn't Know. The track was set on repeat. There was a fluffy pillow beneath my head and magically, Boston had turned into a cozy throw.

"Boston," I called out.

When there was no answer, I headed straight to the kitchen hoping to find… potatoes. There were none.

The note on the table read, "Thanks for everything."

Lineage

Let's just see. It had better be at least $20,000, I thought to myself.

Okay, here we go. The made for TV slot machine style digits started to rumble. There aren't enough spaces up there on that little screen. They're going to bullshit her.

I was lying in bed with my daughter. It was late night. We'd both had our baths and were relaxing, sharing Oprah. She's only four years old. As beautiful as she could be. From a line of wonderfully beautiful people. All humanly flawed. I laid there admiring her. Wishing I could go through her mind and her body and pluck any flawed characteristics from her being. Wishing I could clean up this world so that she may some day fly free... as she was meant to be.

Then, the numbers stopped.

$8,000. $8,000!!!!

Oprah was slow to respond. What in the hell can she say to that, I thought. I know she has to feel it. The humiliation. Family heirlooms from the mid 1800's. Passed on through generations. $8,000. Horrible 20th century paintings went for $40,000. Paintings that didn't possess any of the qualities that would warrant such expensive prices. No extraordinary skills nor techniques demonstrated, no unparalleled levels of creativity. Nothing. Needlework appraised at $30,000. This is some bullshit! Just as I felt myself begin to get pissed, I, the world renown art broker had to deal with reality. Hell, I probably couldn't get nearly that much for those pieces, not even from my wealthiest clients. We don't even value our own treasures. A good piece of art that depicts an experience or somehow relays cultural strength or social conviction will bring you much more gratification than a pair of shoes, a fancy outfit, an expensive watch or even a car. Art caters to the soul.

There are only a few artists who can command the type of money they deserve. WAK is one of them. That's only because he insisted on his work being valued as it should be. He has natural, God given talent which he was fortunate to tap into at a young age. He was the first African-American artist to achieve commercial success painting pictures which featured African-American men and women in sensual/erotic poses and settings.

He makes muscles and brown skin look like a fine serving of TiraMisu. Chocolate to just melt in your mouth. What I most admire about his work is his commitment to creating pieces that celebrate rather than denigrate the sensuality of Black Kings and Queens. Though he had great brothers and sisters like Charles White, Paul Goodnight, Ernie Barnes and Annie Lee leading the way, leaving doors cracked open for him, he was bold enough to step out and follow his heart with a style that was all his own. A style that was different and therefore somewhat controversial. He damn near starved to death while trying to establish himself as an artist to be taken seriously. I remember when he ate cheeseburgers on credit. Talk about paying dues. I saw first hand why they call them "starving artists."

He's eating now, that's for sure, and he clearly understands his role. He's careful not to close the doors behind him as he travels on his way widening the road for artists like Doyle, UpJohn, Fred Matthews and Ulysses Jacobs. These brothers are off the hook. They pour their hearts into their work. They're awesome.

The African-American Art Movement of today is really just a millennium version of the Black Arts Movement from back in the day, The Harlem Renaissance. Everything just sort of recycles itself from generation to generation. Today, like yesterday, we as a people just don't value ourselves nor do we recognize our own potential. If a painting is being sold at a fancy, white owned gallery for $40,000 and I offer to sell a brother the exact painting, not a replica or reproduction, the exact painting that is in the gallery on the wall for $30,000 because I can buy it at a brokers' discount for $25,000, knowing that the gallery probably bought it for $10, 000 (because they got it from a starving African-American artist), believe it or not, the Negro purchasing the piece would rather give the white gallery owner $40,000 than to fathom the idea of putting that amount of money in the hand of a person bearing a Black face. It just messes up their psyche. It instantly decreases the value. They think. Sounds crazy, but it's real. And we pass this foolishness down, from generation to generation.

Sometimes, I wish I could just travel through time. Go back in Arnold Schwarzenegger's body and beat the hell out some people. Thieves who robbed us of our pride. I would just whip... their... asses! I'd just be a big, crazy, white man walking around serving ass-whippings to ignorant white people and to a few sell-out house Niggas, too. Yeah, I would.

"Ooooohhh, weee!"

As hard as I tried to get mad, I couldn't. I couldn't really blame Oprah or her appraisers. They were just mirroring society's reality.

My thoughts were getting too heavy. This was personal. I didn't choose to involve myself, but somehow somebody somewhere some time ago made it personal for me. Life kept me reminded. I'd been discriminated against many times. Not just by people clothed in a skin color unlike my own but also by people who were born of the same master's brew or hue. History's hand had written colored folks a debt which guaranteed an eternity of too little, too late payments. Or so it seems. The reality of my unwanted and unwarranted inheritance sometimes gets to be too much for me. This was one of those times. I could feel my head start to pound. Now it was up to me to decide if I would let this mess screw up my entire night... beautiful beginnings and all.

I don't think so.

I could see something in Oprah's face. She said to the woman, "Keep them, I wouldn't part with them." She repeated that statement a couple of times. My mind translated that to say, I'm sorry and screw 'em, in one smooth subliminal breath. Somehow I just knew that was how she felt. Just as I felt. A tear set idly in my heart. My eyes couldn't cry. I had seen it too many times. Instead I opted to free myself and my mind. I reached over on the side of my bed and grabbed my box. The box Spring had left me.   I took my time and read the poems.   Smiling Eyes.

Smiling Eyes

I see the daisy in a field of weeds
I wish I could fill everyone's needs
I enjoy dancing half-naked in the mirror with me
ninety percent of the time I'm free
Me and my smiling eyes

I see the rainbow in the midst of a storm
I pick up roses despite the thorns
I celebrate things others mourn
The Angels rejoiced the day I was born
Me and my smiling eyes

I like to take one day at a time
I'm simple minded, I like poetry that rhymes
I smile at my reflection and think damn girl, you're fine
To negative things, I'm partially blind
Me and my smiling eyes

I don't usually cry about bills
I understand that excess kills
Love is the only thing I'll leave in my will
with occasional memories to give you thrills...   *courtesy of*
                    Me and my smiling eyes
                            Peace.

How Spring-ish? That was the poem that summed her up. That's was supposed to be the title of her book of poetry. If I could be half the woman she was, I will have accomplished a great thing. I read the poems to my daughter, careful to pick ones that wouldn't be too heavy for her little mind. *Breezes, Bud, fowl play, Soul Power, Soulmate...* as I read *Kiss*, I noticed Tysa was asleep. I kissed her on her forehead and continued reading.

Reading Spring's poetry always relaxed me. *Lord Have Mercy, Treasured Games, Charity functions, Easy Money...* It was amazing how these poems could easily be applied to my life as well as the lives of almost every woman I knew. Then came the difference, "She." The poem that sort of said it all...

SHE
hung with the wrong friends
slept with the wrong men
had unstable next of kin
uncles' demands that wouldn't end
SHE.
found a friend in the pipe
needed things to be alright
had bad days topped with cold, lonely nights
lost her will to fight
SHE... the forgotten one.

That poem was the difference between Spring and most of us. If Spring had the foundation and moral support I had been given, she probably would have been the first woman president or something like that. She was more disciplined than any person

I knew. Afterall, the first year that Spring had consented sex was the same year that I first experienced sex. She had many opportunities, but when given the option, she chose to wait. The difference was not in us, "all people are created equal" is the greatest truth ever written. The difference was in our immediate surroundings... our home environments... our families...

16

Hidden Costs

It was springtime. A time of heavy rainfall. Nature's preparation for new life and beautiful new beginnings.

It was raining. The air was cold and still. I had just celebrated my 16th birthday. Sweet sixteen. It was my first time on an airplane. I wasn't allowed to go across town, in my hometown, Chicago. Yet, here I stood in New York City, in La Guardia Airport, alone. Frightened as I could be, as I was *allowed* to be under the circumstances. My parents couldn't afford to come with me so they did as any responsible parents would do, they sent me. Alone. I had to make the trip. It was their responsibility to provide me the opportunity to have a decent and successful life.

I toted a small, black, borrowed overnight bag whose tattered strap hung over my right shoulder. That way it was easier to carry. I can't remember what I thought about as I moved from the gate to the taxi stand. All I remember is fear. But, I clearly remember the taxi ride.

"St. Lucias, King County Hospital in Brooklyn, please."

"St. Lucias?" the driver repeated.

"Yes."

Everything was dirty and ugly. People were moving

quickly, walking out in front of cars. Drivers were hurrying about, recklessly, totally unlike we were taught in Driver's Ed. I barely saw any Black people. Mostly short, dirty, dingy faced white people. What an ugly place, I thought to myself. I don't think I would want to visit here again. Suddenly, the taxi pulled over.

"Twenty-three dolla."

"O.K."

I looked around trying to spot which building was the hospital. Realizing I hadn't remembered to get the envelope from my sock, I quickly reached down and untied my shoe.

"Twenty-three dolla." The man said again as he peeked nervously into the back seat.

I carefully counted out $23.00. I only had $50 which had to last me the whole trip. I placed the envelope back in my shoe, surveyed the back seat for misplaced belongings, took a deep breath, stepped out of the taxi and into the next ten years of my life.

If I remember correctly, I think it cost my parents about $1200.00. That wasn't including the airfare, new robe, houseshoes and toiletries that were packed in my black bag. That was a lot of money for my family. No doubt, at least one month's rent, car note and good-time money was sacrificed. All to fix Carmen. The procedure itself was more costly back then but mine was even more expensive because I was already nearing the end of my second trimester. I had no idea what that meant and I guess I didn't need to know. Since I was under-age, unemployed and unmarried my mother would make the decision for me. She handled it. It was a mistake. She wasn't really angry with me, just disappointed in me. So everything would be taken care of. The one time I dared question what was happening and expressed that I could feel things moving, I was told that it was just gas because at my stage there was just tissue... a baby had not even really formed yet. This is a very private story but I've got to tell you so that you won't fall prey to ignorance. Ignorance can be a bad thing. Ignorance coupled with fear can be horrid. I don't know that there's anything worse or anything that ruins more lives than fear and ignorance combined. For me, abortion became my method of birth control. I was never taught to be responsible with regards to sex. I was just told not to do it. That doesn't work. But for fear of me having sex, and later for fear of me continuing to have sex, my mother didn't want to discuss it. It was as if we didn't talk about it, it would just go away and leave me alone. Not possible. I was born a sexual creature and so was everyone else walking this earth. It doesn't have to be shameful or scary. I'm sharing this story with hopes that honesty will help to diminish the fear, and allow room for knowledge and education to wipe out the ignorance.

About 9p.m., I lay in the hospital bed thinking. Feeling bad about disappointing my mother. Feeling bad about not telling my boyfriend the truth. My mother had sworn me to secrecy. No one was to know where I was going. No one. She would tell them that I was going on a tour of universities. I had been chosen for some special program because of my grades or something. This story worked perfectly. Afterall, everybody knew that I was very intelligent. As a kid my aunts and uncles nicknamed me "Professor" and teased me relentlessly for being "super smart." I was in honors classes and didn't even have to study. Yeah, we would just say that I went away to see which college I would like to attend. As I began wondering how I could be so smart and yet so dumb that I would end up pregnant, the curtain pulled back and the doctor and a nurse walked in to my tiny space. I wasn't in a room. I was in a bed, behind a curtain on a floor with lots of other girls. All white and all younger than me, with the exception of one woman who was forty-five years old and yes, she too was white.

"Okay, let's see what we have here. When was your last period?" The doctor asked suspiciously as he felt the big bulge in my stomach.

"I'm not sure."

"How far did your doctor say you were?"

"He didn't tell me. He told my mother. He said something about second trimester."

"Well, I think we'd better send her down for confirmation. Just to make sure there were no miscalculations." He smiled. "Tell them to put a rush on this one, she's an out-of-towner and she's scheduled to leave tomorrow."

"Will do," the nurse replied.

After the test was performed, the doctor came back in to see me and informed me that it looked like I made it just in time to be able to have the procedure done.

"It's awfully close but looks like we just can make it. I'm gonna give you a shot here in your navel. It won't be very painful. In a little while you will feel your stomach get tight and it will feel like you've got to go to the washroom. Do not use the washroom. That's very important." He spoke slowly, exaggerating the pronunciation of each word as if I was slow or mentally challenged or something.

I watched him give me the shot with what looked like a 12" needle. Then I was really scared. I didn't want this done. Why hadn't someone asked me? I could make some sacrifices. If only someone would give me the option. I decided to call my boyfriend. He loved me. We were going to be married in a couple of years. He had a right to know. I didn't have any change with me so I called collect. I was praying his parents didn't answer the phone.

"Hello."

"Hi."

"Did that operator say New York?"

"Yep."

"You won't believe what happened today, Carmen. Junior and em' faggot-ass ViceLords came on our side of the tracks and shot at Dennis. I just came home to get my dad's car so we could ride over there and show them that we ain't no punks. They can't just come over here and do whatever, whenever they feel like it. They're pissed because we had a meeting with Blade earlier, trying to work out a truce. Me and Dee told Blade that Black Gangsters run thangs over here. They can ride whatever they want to ride, but they'd better hold that shit on the DL. We don't want to see them representing in our hood or on the main streets that we use. If they want to toss up their flags they need to go out west with them Vickie-Lou's. We ain't having that over here. That's disrespect to the Nation and to Hoover. Blade said they ain't trying to disrespect us, they're just showing love to their people. Dee told him that he'd advise them to take that to their people's hood, and get it off the south side.

We told him that it wasn't a threat, it was just friendly advice. He seemed like everything was cool. Then, next thing I know we hear they rolled on Boo and em' while they were hooping at the park. Then to top it off, I walk in and my parents are sitting in the dining room talking about shipping me off to California to stay with my aunt because the neighborhood is changing. My dad took the keys to his car, but that don't mean nothing. Prescott's got the Cutlass and he's gonna ride out with us. Can you believe he's gonna roll on them with us? I heard he has a couple of gats and everything for us to use. So I've got to hurry up. Don't try to talk me out of it. I'm sick of them marks. We've got to stand up and make them punks respect us. I don't even want to hear you say anything about it Carmen."

There was silence on the phone. He continued.

"What are you doing in New York anyway? I thought you were checking out schools down south."

"I'm not at a school, Shorty. I'm in the hospital."

"What?! What are you talking about?"

"I just told you that because I didn't want you to know where I was going."

"Why?"

"Shorty, I'm pregnant and I'm here to get an abortion."

"Abortion?! But you said the doctor said you weren't pregnant. What?! I can't believe you lied."

"My mother said it would be best if I didn't tell anybody."

"Your mother can't tell us what to do with our baby! You don't have to be there, Carmen. Just leave. Tell them that you don't want this. They can't do it if you say you don't want it.

Your mother can't make you do this. Do you want to do this, Carmen?"

"I don't know. I don't know what to do."

"That's murder! You want to kill our baby? My seed?"

"They said it's not even anything there yet."

"Carmen, listen." He lowered his voice and spoke very slowly. "I love you. I have a right to have a say so. That is my child too, Carmen. Please, just leave."

"It's the middle of the night." I began to cry, regretting my decision to call.

"Where will I go?"

"Go to the airport. It's open 24 hours. There are people there. You'll be safe there, Carmen. Then just come home tomorrow."

"And then what? I don't have anywhere to go. We can't pay for the baby to be born. You have to leave for college next year. My mother and em' spent all of their money on this."

"Carmen, Carmen, Carmen. Just listen to me. I'll find a way to take care of both of y'all. We can pay them their money back."

"Plus, I think its too late. The doctor has already given me a shot in my stomach. I'm not even supposed to be out of bed." I began to cry even more.

"Carmen, don't cry."

Just then a nurse at the end of the hall said to me, "You're not supposed to be on the phone."

"I've got to go."

"Okay, but, just do me a favor and ask if its too late. If it isn't, then promise you won't get the abortion."

"Okay, okay, I'll ask. I've got to go."

"Okay, Prescott is blowing for me anyway. I'll try to call you after we take care of these fools. Or you call me or something. Okay."

I lay there for hours listening to the shrieks and cries of pain from the other girls. I would not cry anymore. I had decided. This is what I have to do. It is too late anyway.
There's nothing there really. Forget it. I'll just go through with it. And I won't cry.

After a few hours of sleeping, I woke up to discomfort. Not the type of pain like the others were yelling about, just discomfort.

"Nurse. Nurse."

I considered just getting up going to the washroom myself but I remembered the doctor's words.

"Nurse."

Just then the curtain flew back.

"Yes, what is it?" she snapped.

"I've got to use the bathroom."

"Oh, well you can't do that."

"But, I really have to go. If I can't get up I'm gonna use it on myself."

"Let me see." She raised up the sheets and visually examined me.

"No it's not time yet. Take this bed pan."

She stepped out of site for a second.

"Lift up."

She hurriedly stuffed the cold, stainless steel bowl beneath my butt.

"When you feel you have to go, use it in that. Do not push. If you feel some pushing, press that nurse's button right there by your head." She quickly left.

Later, I felt something coming out. I thought my bowels were moving. I didn't feel pain that I would associate with the screams I had heard all night so I just thought it was nature doing it's thing. The thought of that grossed me out and made me feel nauseous. I was wrong. My mother had been wrong. Everything was all wrong. I heard it and I immediately knew. I heard the sound of something hard hitting that steel pan... something that was formed and developed. Bones. Head, maybe. I lifted up the sheet and I saw limbs. I felt ashamed, betrayed... bad. My mind was numb. Still to this day I feel new pain whenever I think of that night and similar nights that would follow during the next ten years. There was still pressure down there... down near my private... or what used to be private. I calmly pressed the nurses button.

"Yeah?"

"Something came out. Something is in the pan," I said somberly.

"Wait, don't move. Don't push. Doctor!" She yelled.

The doctor hurried in.

"Okay. In just a second, I'm going to need you to push."

I followed all of the orders, did just what I was supposed to as he dug and scraped to get the afterbirth. Without any attempt at being gentle, he dug and scraped and dug and scraped. As if he was still on his mission to destroy. He couldn't have been helping me at that point. No, this was punishment. Punishment for society offering him the position of terminator as the only avenue to fulfill his dreams and greedy ambitions. Punishment for the nightmares that would come with age to rob him of his true grandfatherly experience. I didn't then, but I do now, feel sad for him.

When the doctor was done, after the nurse had finished cleaning up the mess, just before she was to leave, I asked, "Can you tell me what it was?"

She replied. "Why is it that you girls don't want the babies but you always want to know what it was?" She grabbed my pan with what had been my baby in it, and she turned to leave. Just as she was closing the curtain behind her, she grunted, "Boy. It was a boy."

I'll never forget. A single tear escaped my left eye but the rest of that pain I would carry with me for a long time. The next day I took my black overnight bag and other *baggage* full of stuff that they said was included in the cost of the procedure, and I headed home. Though I was allowed to leave, for some strange reason, I felt I hadn't yet paid the total cost for that procedure.

****

If only I had listened to Spring when she tried to give me some of her birth control pills. Instead, I told her that my mother would be disappointed in me if she found out I was on the pill. She would kill me. Plus, Shorty promised nothing would happen. He promised on our love.

Spring had just shrugged her shoulders and said, "Okay. But, love has nothing to do with sex."

Spring knew that at seventeen. Several years later I was

still trying to understand. As it turned out, Spring was right. Shorty apologized again about a year later. Then Tyrone apologized. The next time, Tyrone didn't offer an apology. He said that I should apologize to him. Apologize for assuming he couldn't and wouldn't be a good father and do right by his child. That second time with Tyrone, he didn't even go into the clinic with me. He just dropped me off and told me to page him when I was done with what I felt I had to do.

After that fourth time, Spring took me out for a drink. Hennessey on the rocks. I remember well because I wasn't supposed to have alcohol, but that had become sort of like our tea. We would always chat over Hennessey.

Spring asked me very bluntly, without consideration for my emotions, "Are you being paid to have abortions? If not, are you out of your mind or something?"

"What are you talking about?" I said. "I just don't want a kid right now. Plus, I don't know what's going on with Tyrone. He's been acting weird lately."

"Okay. So did you just figure that out today, or what?"

"No."

"Well, next time why don't you think about all of that first. You are really surprising me. I never figured you for a murderer. And you're so unmoved by the whole thing."

"I'm not unmoved. I just realize that I had to do what I had to do. Why are you tripping on me? I'm not the first person and I won't be the last. All my friends have had em'. Doctor Tolliver had one last year. Hell, the counselor at the clinic said she's had nine of em'."

"Nine abortions? And she told somebody that?"

"Nothing's there but a glob of tissues. It's not murder. Not if you catch it early. You're talking about the other kind."

"Oh, is that right? And just how early did you catch it? Huh?" Spring glanced at me momentarily then fixed her eyes on the ice cubes resting neatly on the bottom of her almost empty glass. "I hope to God it was before nine weeks. At nine weeks that little innocent baby can feel pain. Which means he suffered."

"Baby?!"

"At eight weeks, that baby has a stomach with liver and kidneys that are functioning. They've recorded brain activity at forty days and a heartbeat as early as eighteen to twenty-five days after conception. They make you wait at least that long before they'll service you, don't they Carmen? You know why? That's because your fruit will be ripe for the picking and there will be less chance of it being damaged therefore, they can get top dollar for it."

She continued, "Oh, your counselor didn't tell you that? Don't they at least give you a cut of the money? And your fruit is probably fresh when they deliver it. I think they say there's a center right here in Illinois that buys that little tissue, as you called it. But, I bet they didn't tell you that either."

"They can't do that. That's illegal."

"Girl, come on. You know there is no such thing as illegal when it's about money. What is it? For every two children born, a third one dies by way of abortion. Do you hear what I'm saying? One out of every three children conceived will never see a smiling face. There are four million births a year and 1.5 million abortions per year. Four *thousand* per day. And one heart beating, organ functioning, pain feeling, thumb sucking, glob of tissue is aborted every twenty seconds. And that's just in the United States alone. And guess who's helping them meet their goals. You and your Black sistergirls. All you educated, the 'world-ain't-gonna-hold-me-back', pro choice, too busy to be bothered women. Do you know you're doing exactly what they want you to do. If nothing else gets to you, that should. Do you even know the history behind abortion?"

Spring was speaking in a matter-of-fact tone. She sounded like a teacher or preacher or something. I was captivated by her knowledge and moral convictions. It was as if someone else was sitting there talking to me. That is until a short, pudgy man wearing a cheap purple toned, pin-striped suit with a black, wide brimmed Dobb hat and shiny, black Stacey Adams interrupted her string of words. I hadn't even seen him coming. I was listening to her each and every word intensely. I only noticed him when she'd said, "Not until nine, sorry."

Then, I'd looked up and saw the man whispering in her ear with his hand resting on a spot too low to be considered her back.

"No, Smith. I just can't. Not, until about nine." Her voice had changed. It was softer. Much more compassionate.

"If I'm done before nine, I'll find you."

The man stepped back. I tried not to look at his face. I pretended to sip from my empty glass and fixed my eyes on the buttons that appeared to be escaping the button holes on the front of his jacket. I wondered how they managed to stay right there, half way in, half way out. I wondered if he'd recently gained weight, if the suit was old, or if he'd intentionally bought it like that. At any rate, his reluctance to leave caused me to look up into his face. I was hoping to somehow cause him to be embarrassed. Then maybe he would go on his way. Though Spring continued to speak softly I could sense that she was becoming irritated and I didn't want any trouble.

His face was round. His eyes were sunken back in the fullness of his face, but I could still see the longing in them. They were begging. Pleading. Spring wasn't even looking at him. I don't think she looked at him once the whole time. I felt sad for him and disgusted by him. He was so emotional, unlike I'd imagined her tricks to be.

Without looking at him, Spring had cupped her hand and rubbed his left arm.

"Nine, Smith. I'll make it up to you at nine."

With that the man had smiled a half smile, sucked in his belly and went on his way. Then, without hesitation, Spring dove right back into the conversation; attitude, tone of voice and all. Spring was a professional and it was just business, that's all.

"Have you or any of your degree holding friends ever heard of eugenics? That came from a man named, Sir Frances Galton, a scientist. Have you ever heard of Margaret Sanger? The lady who made it all possible for you. The lady who founded Planned Parenthood, the largest and most influential abortion provider. She was one who publicly agreed with Hitler's white supremacist ideas. She was quoted as having talked about stuff like, *'the extermination of human weeds… the segregation of morons, misfits, and the maladjusted, and… the sterilization of genetically inferior races'*. That would be you and your glob, Carmen. It isn't an accident that black women get abortions proportionately three times more than white women. In 1939, this chick Sanger organized her *Negro Project* designed to eliminate you. The centers were strategically placed in Negro neighborhoods. She took good care of us. It was all a population control tactic cleverly disguised as a woman's rights issue. Having said all of that, it still boils down to unnecessary drama. If you don't want children, don't have children. I understand that. But at least be responsible enough to handle your business. You aren't in Ethiopia. You don't have to get an abortion because of lack of access to birth control. Did you know that fifty percent of deaths of teenage girls in Nigeria are results of unsafe abortion situations? And you've got all kinds of birth control all around you..."

I sat there amazed and confused. Who was the bad person here? Where was the lesson in all of this? How could she judge me? But, she had. And she was right. But, she was wrong herself. How? Why did she even care, considering her own circumstances? I couldn't make sense of it all. I just wanted her preaching to stop. Her voice coupled with her own reality was starting to irritate me.

"Okay, Spring. I got it. I got it," I said.

I don't know if she could sense my irritation or if she even cared. But she sat there for a moment and then, bam! She hit her hand on the bar. Suddenly, we were back from the classroom of Spring's mind. Back in the half empty lounge. Spring got the attention of the bartender who was standing nearby.

"Tell Spacey to play that song he played the other night, *Miracle.*"

The song she requested was a tune off of Whitney

Houston's not yet released, new album. DJ Spacey was well connected. He often got new songs before they hit the market.

The words of the song spoke directly to me. The melody was slow and soulful. The words were clear. The song was draining me. I was depressed. Spring, who always thought she was Whitney anyway, began singing.

"Thought I was looking out for myself. Now it seems the pain is all that I have gained. I wonder if I could be your miracle. I wonder if I could spare you pain. Seems as though nothing will comfort me. Less today, When I pray. That you should come listen..."

Spring hit that high note. I swear she sounded just like Whitney. She smiled proudly and threw her hand up for high five. I had to give it to her, the high five. She nailed it. As the song came to an end she smiled again and threw one arm around my neck, holding me in a choke hold only Hennessey could have led her to believe was okay. Then she yelled towards the hole cut-out in the plywood wall which was covered in imitation brick, the DJ booth, "Can we get some LeVert, Rope-a-Dope Style?"

DJ Spacey obliged. How I wished he hadn't. The music took control of Spring. She jerked back and forth, swinging her hips side to side, with our buddy Hennessey in one hand and my neck in the other. She held both of us for dear life as she egged herself on as if no other people were in the room... "The roof! The roof! The roof is on fire, we don't need no water..."

17

Thanksgiving

"Excuse me. Can I help you with something?"

"Aw, no. I'm just having a look. Checking out y'all's place. I'm gonna check you out in a few, big fella."

He's gonna check me out? Tyson thought to himself. I don't want him to check me out. I don't even know why he's here. I can't wait until my dad gets here. All these strange people are in our house. Why couldn't Marcus just go to one of their houses or why didn't all of them meet wherever they met last year. It's too crowded in here.

"C'mon big fella. Watchu working with in here? Got some Power Rangers or something? I know you got you one of those cowboy sets. Give me a gun and I'll play witcha."

The man stumbled as he reached for the basketball on the shelf.

"Is this here real?"

"Yes." Tyson answered.

"Who bought this for you?"

I'm not even going to answer this man. Maybe he'll go away. Where is my mom? She doesn't even allow grown-ups to come up here, in our rooms. I wish she would come get this man with his stinky breath and shiny hair out of here.

The man licked his finger and began to rub it back and

forth over one of the signed names on the basketball.

"Is this real? Real NBA players signed this theyself?"

Theyself? Tyson thought to himself as he reached and grabbed the basketball.

"Yeah!"

"How do you know? People tell kids anything."

"I went in the locker room after a game and got all the players to sign it." Tyson said with a pinch of irritation in his voice.

"How'd you get back there? You sneak in?" The man leaned towards Tyson when he spoke. His breath was stinky, like a skunk mixed with medicine or peppermints.

"Uhm... Excuse me, but could you please wait for whoever downstairs? I'm not allowed to have company in my room."

"Aw, okay, big fella. No problem. It ain't like I'm gonna steal nothing. It's cool though."

He stumbled out into the hallway and made his way down the stairs. Assured the man was gone for good, Tyson sat on the floor near the bottom of his bed and began playing his Play Station 2.

"Ding-dong." Tyson tried to block the sound of the doorbell out of his head as he gripped the controller tighter.

"Ding-dong. Ding-dong."

Tyson reluctantly put the game on pause, carefully laid the controller on the floor and hurried to answer the door before Carmen would be forced to come all the way up from the basement. She would surely be angry about that.

As Tyson got halfway down the staircase, Marcus

appeared and opened the door.

Tyson stood watching as he wondered who else could possibly fit into his already filled to capacity home.

"Hey, how y'all doing?" Marcus asked as he greeted Carla with a hug. As Marcus stepped out of the doorway, in ran Randy, Raynard and Toshanna. Then came Emil, Carla's friend Paula's son.

"Hey, everybody." Marcus continued happily as he started to close the door.

"Wait! Can I come in? Is the party over?" Paula joked as she pushed through the door.

"Sorry bout' that, baby."

"No, that's okay. I wasn't worried about it. I knew I would get in, cause ain't no party without me." Paula laughed loud. "Careful, Marcus. This coat is soaked. Emil's bad butt was jumping around like a jackrabbit and fell in the mud. I blasted the heat in the car hoping it would dry, but..."

"Oh, no problem. Kids will be kids," Marcus said as he took the jacket. "We're going to put this right here so that it's out of the way." Marcus laid the soaked coat on the arm of the living room couch.

"Are you sure, Marcus? It's still pretty wet."

"Woman if you don't get in there and have some fun and stop worrying me about this jacket... you'd better."

Paula smiled and headed towards the music and noise in the dining room.

If my mom sees that coat, that wet coat on her suede couch, she is going to snap off. Marcus acts as if he thinks he's running stuff. He doesn't live here, Tyson thought to himself as he waved his hand motioning to the kids to come upstairs. The kids followed quickly and they all disappeared into Tyson's room.

****

"Man, I'm just saying…"

"No, you're right. I know exactly what you're saying. Wait one second. Tyson!" Marcus called. "Tyson!!"

"One minute," Tyson responded as he lifted the controller higher and concentrated on what could be the last play of the game.

"See what I'm saying, man. Ain't no kid supposed to be talking to a grown man like that. You'd better nip that in the bud, man." The grown-up man slurred.

"No! Not in a minute. Right now!" Marcus yelled.

"Okay, okay," Tyson pleaded. "It's almost over."

"Tyson! I said now!" Marcus yelled.

The kids dived toward the controller as Tyson dropped it and headed out the door. Marcus stood at the bottom of the stairs with one arm extended on the railing.

"What is your problem tonight?"

"Nothing. I was just trying to finish the game."

"Nate says you were rude and disrespectful to him."

"Nate? Who is Nate?"

Just then the stranger stepped into view. He stood with shoulders slumped forward leaning to one side.

"Tyson, don't play with me," Marcus snapped.

"I didn't know who you were talking about. I didn't

know his name."

"You know who you were disrespectful to. Don't talk to me like I'm crazy."

"I didn't say anything bad to him."

"You talked to me like I was a kid or something. I ain't no kid. You need to learn to respect your elders."

"What?" Tyson's asked.

"No, not 'what'! You know exactly what he's talking about. You're a kid and you'd better act like one! Do you hear me?! This is a grown man. You don't just talk to him any way you want to!"

"Yeah, cause if Marcus wasn't here, I'd whip your butt myself."

Nate's head lifted up as his eyes rolled around desperately, trying to land on Tyson's real image. Tyson seemed to be playing tricks on Nate, as three or four Tysons appeared and disappeared, then appeared and disappeared again and again.

Tyson looked puzzled.

Marcus yelled, "And don't look like that. You think I'm playing. That's your problem, you think everything is a joke."

Raynard held the railing as he peeked around the corner from the upstairs landing.

"Tyson, Randy just got you out."

Marcus stared at Tyson. "As a matter of fact, you're done playing the game for tonight, since you don't know how to act."

"But, I..."

"But I what? You're gonna learn your place, one way or another."

"I didn't even say anything to him. I..."

Having heard the yelling, Randy and Emil walked out of the room to watch the commotion.

"See look at you. You still ain't learning nothing. I don't want to hear a sound from you the rest of the night. Now you apologize!"

Tyson stood at the top of the stairs crying. He could ignore Marcus and his drunk pal but Play Station was a whole different story.

"And I don't care about your crying. I ain't your mama. You can't run that bullcrap on me. Now apologize! APOLOGIZE NOW!"

"Sorry," Tyson mumbled through short, sobbing breaths.

"What is wrong with you?" Carmen questioned as she suddenly appeared at the bottom of the steps and saw Tyson crying.

"He's okay. He's just spoiled, that's what's wrong with him. But we gonna fix all of that." Marcus spoke sharply as he stood staring at Tyson.

"What happened, Tyson? Come here," Carmen said.

Still crying, Tyson slowly walked down the stairs.

"Now, I'm not going to ask you again, Tyson."

"Marcus said I was being rude to that man, but I wasn't."

"So why are you crying? You just tell them that there must be a mistake and that you didn't intend to be rude." Carmen spoke matter-of-factly as she put her hand underneath Tyson's chin and lifted his head.

The area was quiet momentarily. Then, a big lady with an even bigger voice made her way towards the door.

"We gonna have to get out of here y'all."

"You gone?" Marcus asked as he turned to hug the big lady.

"Yeah, I'm tired. We've been visiting all day. We're gonna head home now. But thank y'all for having us."

"No problem, you know you're always welcome in my house," Marcus replied as he place one hand on the lady's shoulder. "Y'all get some food to take home?"

"We got a lil sumn'. Couple of plates."

"You got enough? You sure? Help yourself. We don't need all that food. Get some more of that turkey."

Carmen looked at Marcus.

"Well, I guess we could. Big Joe get a couple more plates of dressing and yams. Get you some of that macaroni and cheese too. That way you won't have to come over and ask me for mine. And fix your mama and Beanie plates, too. We'll be in the car. It was nice meeting you, Carly. Call me Marcus." The lady said as she, two other adults and three children grabbed their plates full of food from the living room couch and lined up to give Marcus hugs as they exited the house.

"Carmen," Carmen said in an irritated voice as she leaned back against the wall with one arm resting on Tyson's shoulder.

When the last guy in line reached the door Marcus began laughing and speaking loudly.

"Okay, man. What's your name again? I'm going to be looking for you on game days. Bring some friends too, cause I'm telling you who's gonna take it this year."

Marcus gave the red-eyed man the soul brother

handshake/hug and then turned to speak to Carmen who was staring at him blankly with her mouth slightly open. "And you stop babying him. He's gonna learn that, yes there are rules and there are consequences to acting like a fool."

"What?" Carmen asked although she had clearly heard each word Marcus said.

"What did he say to the man?"

"The *man's* name is Nate and it doesn't matter what he said. Nate is a grown man and Tyson disrespected him. I'm not going to have that."

"All I said is that I couldn't have company in my room," Tyson interjected.

"You have company in your room now, Tyson. What do you call those kids in there now? Huh? Huh?!"

"Kids. I can't have grown people in my room."

"And he told him right. Who was he with up there? Why was he in a kid's room? Go on upstairs Tyson." Carmen waved her finger back and forth towards the stairway. "He's not here to visit Tyson. The party is down here. He's your friend, he should be with you."

Nate interjected, "That ain't all you said. Stop lying."

"I'm not telling a story. I..."

"Be quiet Tyson and go on upstairs. And uh, what's your name again?'

"My name is Nate," the man said with an attitude.

"Nate, please don't call my son a liar. I'm sorry if he offended you, but Tyson was just doing and saying what he's been taught."

"So he's taught to be rude?" Marcus pressed.

Carmen kept her eyes fixed on Nate as she continued. "It wasn't personal. Okay? So, you can just go on back there and enjoy yourself. You want something else to drink?" She snapped sarcastically.

Not even aware that he had been slightly insulted, Nate replied, "I'm just saying, you need to handle that. That boy is family now and ain't no family of mine going to grow up like that. With no manners. The next time I'm going to handle his little mannish ass myself."

"Well, Nate as long as everybody respects my house, there won't be a next time."

"Everybody?" Marcus said, again attempting to work his way back into the conversation. "This ain't everybody! This is my cousin, Nate."

"Cousin Nate, uncle DooLittle, aunt Betsy Ross…I don't want grown motherfuckers in my kids' rooms unless I personally invite them in there." Carmen bobbed her head back and forth as she spit her words out daring Marcus or Nate to make her go there.

"I wasn't going to bother your son, lady."

"You need to stop tripping, Carmen. Sorry about this, Nate. Man, I apologize for the whole thing. Come on, let me fix you a drink."

As Marcus walked away, he looked back at Carmen, rolled his eyes and repeated, "You need to stop. Really. It don't make no sense."

****

Tyson lingered in the hallway between the top of the stairs and the doorway of his bedroom. He'd heard his Mama's comments and felt somewhat vindicated. He wiped the final traces of embarrassment from his face and prepared to enter his room. Tyson frowned as he allowed himself one last thought about Marcus.

How is he going to give away all of our stuff? We already have to move. Does he even know that my mom had to use her last money to buy that food? Does he even care? I was supposed to take turkey sandwiches for lunch all next week. There won't be any leftovers with him letting everybody to take our food. Did he even buy *anything* for today? I bet he didn't. But he's trying to walk around here telling people what to do. If he thinks he's gonna be my dad, he's wrong. I've got a dad and I don't need another one, especially him.

Marcus can't tell me what to do. If I tell my dad how he was talking to me, my dad would crush him. He already doesn't like him. He said he *wished Marcus would*, lay a hand on me or my sister. He would kill Marcus. Plus, if I tell my dad about all these people Marcus brought in our house drinking wine around Tysa, he would... I don't even want to think of what he would do. Tysa is just a little girl. They shouldn't drink in front of her. My mom should just take my dad back. He would never allow any of this kind of stuff. I don't know what he could've done so wrong that she'd rather have Marcus and his drunk friends.

18

Product Inventory

"Hey. Carmen, right? How are you? Come on in. Excuse me for not being dressed properly, I just got out of the shower."

The wide bodied man turned and casually walked his tiger-print boxers to the chair positioned in the middle of the room in direct alignment with the television.

"Have a seat."

Carmen looked at the single, overstuffed, tiger-print chair. A box of cereal was propped against the side. Fruit Loops, maybe. A video game box with two controllers lay in the center of the floor. Near the front of the chair, there were three or four remote controls which apparently enabled Nuk as Amy had called him, to operate the many black boxes strategically placed in compartments built in the wall around the huge television screen.

Near the back of the chair Carmen noticed the jars of peanut butter and jelly. The lid of the peanut butter jar was about three inches, no, two inches from the tip of Carmen's wintergreen, suede , wedge-heeled boot. Carmen eased her foot away from the lid hoping Nuk hadn't noticed.

"No, thank you."

Carmen smiled a polite smile.

"I don't have much time. I have another appointment at eight. Amy explained your situation to me. She said you were a special buddy of hers and she requested that I give you prompt attention. She said that you were in dier need."

Again, Carmen smiled her polite smile.

"I thought I'd get some pictures and measurements so that we could get the ball rolling. I brought a few books with me."

Carmen squatted down to balance the her briefcase on her thighs as she retrieved the photo albums.

"Here you are, have a look at these so that I can get a sense of what you like."

Carmen looked up towards Nuk. To her surprise, he was seated in the chair. She was blown away! His loose fitting boxers were blabber-mouths. Their rims held no secrets. They were spilling it all, every bit of his business. Carmen was instantly knocked off balance by the embarrassment. She began to fall backwards. Nuk's strong arm, reached out, anchored like an I-Beam in a permanent structure, and caught her just in the nick of time.

"Oh, goodness... my mind keeps forgetting to remind my legs that I'm not twenty-five anymore. So, anyway, like I was saying, have a look at these and let me know which styles and colors you find to be pleasing to..."

Carmen paused briefly. She needed to pick her words carefully. Nuk seemed to be paying more attention to her perfectly tailored slacks and the way they rested on her hips, than her pictures, her conversation or anything else pertaining to business.

Here we go again. Carmen thought to herself as she looked around the empty room trying to decide what measurements were absolutely mandatory.

She had just arrived and yet, she was already trying to leave. Carmen had instructed the tailor to give her a cut that would hide the goods without making her look dopey. The slanted-eye tailor had laughed profusely when Carmen had poked her index fingers into her hips repeatedly while imitating his broken English, "No see. No see. No see. Gone. Vanish. Disappear. Secret. No sell this. Get it? Hide."

The tailor had responded with raised eyebrows and a smile as he rolled his eyes and shook his head from side to side.

"No hide. No hide. Sah-we."

Nuk seemed to be in complete agreement with the tailors thoughts, there was no hiding place for Carmen's hips.

"Is it okay if I go around and take a few pictures?"

"Help yourself. Whatever you want to do."

Nuk sat still. His boxers were still running at the mouth, telling all of his secrets. Carmen quickly left the room and preceded to handle her business. When she returned a few minutes later, she was moving and talking quickly as if she herself believed she had another appointment.

"Okay, Sir... Did you find anything appealing in any of the books?"

Carmen pointed to the photo albums stacked neatly on the floor near the cereal box right where she'd left them.

"I've got some great ideas for the dining area and the den. Were you wanting to accentuate that Maplewood trim? Do you like it? Or, were you wanting to down play it so that it's barely noticeable?"

Carmen was uneasy with this guy, Nuk. Nuk was big. Nuk was quiet. His eyes and his underpants were speaking boldly but no words came from his mouth. This made Carmen nervous. She was trying hard to suppress her anxiety. She needed the job. She needed the money and somehow she felt Nuk knew all of that.

Nuk spoke.

"I saw something that I liked, but it ain't in no book."

Carmen lifted her camera and began to take pictures of the room.

"Was it in a gallery or furniture store?"

"Naw."

Nuk's voice startled Carmen. He was up out of the chair and had eased in close behind her.

"It was right here." He gently placed his hands on Carmen's waist.

"No, I think you'd better look at the books."

Carmen stepped away and continued snapping pictures.

"I really have to go and I need to know what you would like to have done *in your home*."

Carmen was angry. She spoke in a clear manner. She was careful to enunciate her words properly as she often did when attempting to control her anger.

"Well, you got your pictures. We can talk about the rest later, can't we? Right now, I want to talk about you. Why don't you skip that appointment and let me take you to dinner. I'll pay you whatever money you miss."

Carmen stood staring at him. Nuk continued.

"Money ain't a thang, baby. I've got checks, and don't worry, they rolling right through the banks. So, we don't need to press this thang right now."

"Well actually, we do. I have three projects scheduled for the first of the year. I really need to get started on your home now, if you want it done anytime within the next year."

"Whatever. Tell me Carmen, What will it take for me to take you to dinner?"

"Thanks. I really appreciate your offer, but I have to make this other appointment. Do you have a preference as to what is placed in your home?"

"I sure do."

Nuk stood staring at Carmen.

"Can you tell me what it is?"

Carmen flipped the pages of the photo albums pausing at various artists styles.

"This is abstract. I think it would look great over the fireplace. Have you chosen furniture? Do you know your color scheme? I can commission an artist to create a piece with any subject matter and practically any colors. I work with several artists, excellent artists."

Nuk was sitting down. He stared blankly at Carmen.

Carmen pressed on.

"Would you like to look at the work of some other artists I deal with? Did you want to possibly meet at The Mart tomorrow to have a look at some furniture?"

"Nope."

"Is there a problem or a misunderstanding here?"

Carmen pleaded.

"Ain't no problem. I'm just wondering how long it's gonna take you to do what you gotta do with me, so that I can do what you want me to do with you. Then, you can have your little check and do your thang. I'm not getting in to all of this bull right now. First things first. You come on and quit playing all hard and uh, then we'll talk business."

"What do you mean?"

"I think you know what I mean. We can go ahead and get this out of the way, then the rest is gravy. I definitely like your style and I plan to do business with you, but..."

Carmen couldn't believe what she was hearing. She had previous clients who had attempted to date her, or screw her, whatever the case may have been but never had anyone been as direct as Nuk.

"Excuse, me? Did I get my times confused? On this job, my day job, I sell art. Pussy is my midnight product, and right now I'm sold out of that. But I'd like to assist you in beautifying your home with some of our fine art products."

Nuk's eyebrows raised slightly.

"Is that right? Yeah?" Nuk asked.

He smiled.

"Well, I think I'll wait. You give me a call when you get some of that other product in your inventory and then maybe we can talk about the art."

He got up from the tiger-print chair and went into the kitchen.

Carmen stuffed her albums and paperwork into her briefcase. As she walked towards the door, she was met by Nuk who came around the other side from the kitchen.

He opened the door, stepped to the side and said, "Don't forget to let me know when you get some of that in."

Carmen told herself not to say anything to him. She badly needed that check.

Maybe this was just a test. Maybe he was just trying her to see if she'd give in. He might feel guilty and call her back. He might even apologize and then give her the check. She could feel him watching her as she walked away. She was so glad that her coat was long. She couldn't stomach the thought of him watching her ass swing side to side. She was sure the coat camouflaged her well.

Just as she got to her car which was parked in the circular drive, Nuk shouted, "If you change your mind, give me a call."

"Asshole!!" Carmen thought to herself. She yelled back, "Don't hold your breath!" Then she mumbled, "Fat-ass, ignorant bastard!"

She was careful to keep her voice low. She hadn't given up on the possibility that he may have a change of heart. He couldn't be that ruthless. On the drive home, Carmen cried. She was embarrassed. She was mad. She was hurt. She was tired.

19

Issues

I can't understand why Carmen gets so upset. God knows I love that woman. I wish she wouldn't let every little thing bother her.

Last night, twelve days before Christmas, she lay in bed crying. She told me they were going to take her house. She asked if I could come over, said she needed to talk to me. Well, I had already committed myself to going over to my buddy's friend's father's house to have a couple of drinks with his friend's old man. It wasn't a big deal or nothing, it's just that I'm a man of my word. When my buddy told me where he was going, I asked if he thought they would mind if I came along. He said he thought it would be cool. Then Carmen called wanting me to come over. When I told her I had a couple of things to do, she seemed irritated. I told her I would stop by after I was done. She was mad, I know she was. But whatever. Carmen is just spoiled. She's used to all those rich guys catering to her every whim. It's ridiculous. You should have heard her crying last night. At first I thought she was laughing.

"You always have to help somebody," she said. "How about helping me for a change?"

That's when I knew she had lost her mind. I'm always

helping her. Moving, assembling or fixing something everyday. Then while I was talking to J. Bones' friend's dad, she called my cell phone and asked me what time I thought I'd be done.

Sometimes Carmen gets confused. She talks to me as if she's talking to Tyson or somebody. I had already told her when to expect me. Her calling was her way of forcing me to do what she wanted, when she wanted. Well, it didn't work..

"Didn't I say I'd be there when I'm done?"

Once she saw her little gimmick wasn't going to work, she started that crying mess again. She is so spoiled. I'm going to have to break her of that. The crying stuff wasn't normal for her but I recognized it for what it was, an attempt to control me. So I just let her cry. For her own good, I let her cry. Then I told her she had to just wait until I could get there and she needed to stop being such a brat.

That's when she came with the house stuff. As if that was the reason for the drama.

"Marcus, are you listening? They're going to take the house!"

"I heard you when you told me the first time. And like I told you, we'll take care of it. Stop worrying so much. It isn't like we don't have a place to go. We can stay at my mother's house in my room. We'll deal with this later, Carmen."

"How in the hell will all of us stay in your room at your mother's? I don't want to stay at your mama's house, Marcus!" Carmen yelled. "You shouldn't even be atcha' damn mama's house."

"Carmen, calm down. Everything is going to be alright."

"Everything is not alright! There are problems in the

world, Marcus. Problems in our lives. We are grown people with grown issues! And difficulties! And conflicts! You need to try and help fix some of this shit, Mr. Fix It, helpful ass motherfucker!"

She tried to yell but the crying caused her to be short of breath and the words came out short and choppy. All that drama, because I wouldn't come over when she wanted me to. I know that's all it was.

I firmly told her, "Carmen, I am out with friends and I'll talk to you about this later. Now you get yourself together."

By the time I got to her house, about 3am, she looked terrible. She'd been awake almost twenty-four hours everyday for about a week. Her eyes were red and puffy with dark circles around them. Her curls were smashed flat on one side and her hair looked matted like one of those homeless people you see downtown. She was very quiet, kind of mysterious and crazy acting. She sort of reminded me of that actress in Martin Lawrence's movie, *Thin Line Between Love and Hate.*

I tried to talk to her and explain that I can't be with her every second of every day. Sometimes I'm going to hang with my buddies and she's going to have to understand that. She laughed. That scared me. I know she laughed to make me think it was no big deal. In an instant she cut the laughter, almost in one breath, and her face was blank and serious.

"What about your bonds," she asked.

I thought to myself, I know she ain't asking me to spend that money. I've had those bonds for years.

"Those bonds are not to be used. They are for emergencies - rainy days."

She had a crazy look on her face when she spoke.

"Marcus, it's a fucking monsoon... don't you see shit flooded all around us? We're drowning, Marcus. How much damn rain do you need? Huh, sweetie? We're going to lose the house."

Oh, we're going to lose the house. I thought to myself. So now it's our house.

20

Dollars and Sense

When I got up this morning it was already 9:30. I stayed overnight, here at Carmen's. I was up late thinking about the whole house mess. Wondering if I should put my life savings into saving a house.

I heard Carmen when she walked past me early this morning. It must have been about six or seven o'clock. I just laid there, pretending to be sleep, until I actually fell back to sleep. I didn't want her to start nagging me again about the house and the money and the wedding and everything else. I had a couple of errands to run, so when I woke up and realized she was gone, I got up and got out.

****

I got up early this morning. I can't rest with all of this on my mind. I need to get out and try to get something. I've got to find a way to work things out. It pissed me off when I got up at 5:30 in the morning, went down to fix breakfast and Marcus was lying there on the couch resting peacefully, as if he didn't have a care in the world. Then after I got the kids off to school, cleaned up, took out the trash, took a shower, got dressed, and got on the phone trying to schedule interviews anywhere that may have been hiring, I go downstairs and Marcus' big ass is still lying there. Ain't moved a muscle. Sprawled out on my $6500 suede couch, feet and all. He was probably hung over from last night.

I went into the dining room and searched through my CD collection. I was trying to find that song, the dusty that says, *"Go away, little boy... Why don't you just go away, little boy... you see I am not supposed to sit up here in the dark with some mirrors and no money and no you..."*

I was going to put it on and blast the part that says, *"When I get up to go to work, every able body in the household is supposed to get up and go... at least looking!"*

I searched and searched for the CD. I was so upset, I couldn't remember who sang the song nor could I remember which greatest hits CD it was on. That just made me more pissed.

I can't understand how a man so fine and kind can be so worthless. I must admit, he wasn't looking as fine to me as he used to. Nothing about him has been turning me on lately. He was starting to look fat. He's been too lazy to even work out. I'll bet after we're married he's going to be a wobbly mess. A fat, lazy ass mess. Just sucking me dry. If he had something else to contribute, maybe I wouldn't even think about him getting out of shape. I've gotten a little thick lately myself, but broke, lazy and fat and sloppy? Hell, no!

****

It was late evening when I finally spoke with Carmen. She was probably feeling bad about the things she said last night.

I'm glad I didn't say anything to her this morning. I know she's been a little stressed. All she probably needed was a little time to relax. I knew she'd be calling sooner or later. She called while I was in my guy's store.

"Hi, Marcus."

"Hello, Ms. Carmen."

"Where are you?"

"At my buddy's store."

"Oh. I was just checking to see if you were coming over for dinner tonight?"

"I guess I can. Would you like me to?"

"It's up to you. I just need to know so that I can fix enough food."

"If you want me to come over, I'll come over. That's not a problem, Carmen."

The phone was silent for a few moments. Then Carmen spoke.

"So, what type of store does your friend have? Is it somebody you went to school with?"

"No. No, I met this guy by coming in to his store a while ago. He owns this pawn shop right off of 35th Street. He's a good guy. He cuts me great deals. He looks out for me."

"So, you're just hanging out, huh?"

"Well, I stopped by to pay on my layaway. I didn't realize what today's date was until a couple of hours ago. The payment is due today. I've never been late with a payment. I don't want to start making late payments or none of that craziness now. You know what I mean Mrs. Martin? That sounds good doesn't it? Mrs. Martin. I'm gonna have to call you that regularly now. So you can get used to it."

"Yep. So, what did you buy?" Carmen inquired.

"I got this tool set. It was a steal. At Sears, the same set would have been about $250. My guy gave it to me for $125."

"Yeah? For only $125?" Carmen added sarcastically.

"Uhnn, huh," Marcus replied proudly. "I've only got two more payments. You know? I just give him $25 every two weeks. I could have paid $10 each payment but I just wanted to go ahead and knock it out. Get it out of the way, you know?"

"Yep, Marcus, I think I do." Carmen spoke slowly.

"So, what time is dinner? I got good news to tell you, anyway."

"Well, I'm cooking now."

"What are you fixing?"

"Spaghetti with ground turkey, garlic bread and baked chicken. I should be done around seven."

"Okay, I've got a couple of stops to make and I should be there around eight or eight-thirty."

"Stops?"

"Yeah. I'm going to roll past my boy's house down here on the low end. Then I'll probably go by the house to put the mail inside. You know my mother is at Bible Study almost all day on Wednesdays, she won't be home for another hour or so. I don't want to leave the mail in the box that late. It just doesn't look good, you know."

"Oh, yeah?"

"Yeah. Don't worry, I shouldn't be too long. You must be missing me," Marcus teased.

"Bye, Marcus. I'll see you when you get here."

****

Carmen held the receiver even though it was securely in it's wall mount.

Sometimes, I wonder if Marcus is slow. I mean really, mentally slow. Maybe he could apply for some type of government check. He can't be real. Twenty-five dollar payments? Plus, he's only going to use the tools to do free, buddy-buddy work. I don't know how this is gonna work. This can't be normal.

****

"The dinner was delicious, Carmen. You know I love your spaghetti."

"Thank you. So, what was the surprise you had for me? The good news?"

"Wellll... I know money is tight, but we'll only be married once. We've got to do this right. You remember my guy Eddie? Steady Eddie, down at the pool hall. You remember him. Anyway, he introduced me to this young lady who works with the airline. She's a sweet girl. She does this thing where she can transfer other people's frequent flyer credits to your frequent flyer account."

"We don't have frequent flyer accounts. At least, I don't. Do you?"

"Just be quiet for a minute and let me finish. No, we don't have accounts. But, I had that taken care of. I do take care of things, even though you don't give me much credit. She's going to create accounts under false names and addresses and stuff... would you just wait one minute and let me finish? Then, my guy has this guy Lil' Willie who's gonna hook us up with bogus ID's, and you and me, Mrs. Martin, we're going to honeymoon anywhere in this world your little heart desires."

Carmen was silent.

"My guy said the ID's are almost perfect. We need to give the guy Lil' Willie at least three days to hook em up. Then on the day we want to fly, all I have to do is call the young lady and she'll transfer the miles. I also got a hook-up on hotels."

"What might that be?" Carmen asked. She completed the thought silently in her head, "What now?... just stick a gun to someone's head for a few seconds and force them to give us a luxury suite?.. Hide in the washroom of the bedding store until they close... Watch for an elderly, blind, deaf, senile, person and just sneak into their room because they'd never know... What? Huh? What?"

"This other young lady I know is going to let me use her employee family discount. So, Carmen, there is nothing to worry about. I took care of everything. All you have to do is pick a place, get your half of the money and we're off to paradise."

Again Carmen was silent. Her face was expressionless. Her eyes were fixed on Marcus.

Marcus couldn't figure out what she was thinking.

"This is practically a sure thing, Carmen. If you're nervous about it, we could pick somewhere close. That way if we run into any difficulties with the ticket or the hotel room, we can just rent a car and drive back home. But nothing will probably happen. The only small catch to this whole thing is if we should happen to see one of the ladies who's hooking these deals up, we'll have to say you are my sister."

Marcus smiled a nervous smile.

"I doubt that we'll see either of them, though." He shook his head side to side.

"Why on earth would we have to do that, Marcus?" Carmen asked sarcastically.

Marcus' smile instantly hid itself.

"Well, Carmen everything cost something. You know that. But all that matters, is that we get to take our trip."

"I don't get it, I'm a little slow today. Help me out."

"Well, I think both of them are a little sweet on me. Hell, I don't even bother with that... not at all! I'm just getting us a trip out of the deal."

Carmen stared at Marcus with a puzzled look on her face.

"Nothing transpired between us. A little innocent flirting, that's it. Now, why are you looking like that? I'm trying to do something special for you, Carmen. Don't let your jealousy or insecurities mess things up for us. Okay? Just flow with it."

Carmen didn't respond.

"Well, don't answer now. You've got until tomorrow. Day after tomorrow we have to take pictures down to Lil' Willie to get those ID's made. Let me know where you'd like to go by tomorrow."

Still nothing from Carmen.

"See there, when you let me, I can do some things right."

Marcus smiled, kissed Carmen on the cheek, grabbed his tall glass of Kool-Aid he'd just made and strutted proudly towards the living room.

As he walked away, Carmen watched the red liquid and ice as it played dangerously with the rim of the blue tinted, clear glass which was heading towards her expensive off-white carpet.

She spoke silently to herself, "Did he just make one glass of Kool-Aid? You never make one damn glass of Kool-Aid!"

21

Fair-Weather Friends

"Hello."

"Hi, Emily."

"Hey, Sharon. Girl, I almost didn't answer the phone. I didn't recognize the number. Where are you?"

"In my car. I changed my number. There was a pest that wouldn't stop calling me."

"Who?"

"That fool, Gino."

"The guy from last summer, with the rotten tooth in the front of his mouth?"

"That would be the one."

"I tried to warn you. I told you not to give him none. I knew that brown tooth would haunt you someday. But nooooooo... you had yourself convinced that it wouldn't be a problem."

"Well, the tooth wasn't the problem. It was an unsightly big fella, but believe it or not, I could deal with that. That could have just been replaced. A shiny new white tooth for Christmas or birthday or something. I would have happily paid for that. I wasn't tripping on that. The problem was that sleepy-eye, rotten tooth monster had the audacity to be a damn cheater."

"No!"

"Yes."

"Naw, I don't believe that. Somebody lied on him."

"I saw him myself, Emily."

"I just don't believe that. Maybe, it wasn't what it looked like."

"Yeah, okay."

"So what happened? What did he say?"

"One night I was at the girlie club with some of the guys from the afternoon shift and I saw him there all over his little girlfriend."

"Girl, please! That's what he's supposed to do there. You'd be surprised at the men who go there. You weren't supposed to see that. You weren't supposed to be there. Why were you there anyway?"

"First of all, I go anywhere I damn well please. He wasn't supposed to be doing what he was doing. Don't go and switch that on me. What was I doing there? Hell, what was he doing there? I went with some of the guys from the afternoon shift at work. They dared me to go. They bet me two tickets to the Brian McKnight concert, so yes I did. I sure did strut right up in there."

"Well, what if he would have went off about you being there with those men?"

"Girl, you're talking apples and oranges here. He was all up on the girl, left with the girl hand in hand and stayed at her damn house all night. One of the guys who was with us, knew the girl and commented on how stupid Gino was. He went on and on about how he's paying the girl's bills and everything while she's sexing everybody from here to Jamaica. He said the girl lived in his step brother's building. Her name was Daeh, or something like that."

"Does she live in Hyde Park?"

"No, this girl lived in Calumet City. She was a big, yellow girl who was about one deep breath from being overweight. Her hair was nappy and wild. She had a flat, pie face. She was dressed sort of like a slutty clown or something, wearing who-shot-me, trying to pass as Versace. I don't remember much about her."

"Really? What else was there? Her panty size?"

"That tramp probably wasn't wearing any."

"So, what did he say when you confronted him?"

"I didn't."

"You haven't to this day?"

"No. I paged him a bunch of times that night. I was only calling to tell him not to call me anymore. He wouldn't even call me back so that I could tell him not to call me back. You know what I'm saying? That pissed me off. I sat in the house burning mad until finally I drove over there. Sure enough there was his car. I sat out there and paged him some more. I wasn't sure which building it was or I would have gone to the door."

"No."

"Yes. I thought about sugar in the tank, keys on the paint, knives in the tires... all of that. I was really pissed. How dare that lil skinny, ugly, rotten tooth freak try to play me. Hell, I stepped way outside of my norm to date that monster and he was rotten just like his damn tooth. Paying bills for somebody. Broke ass."

"So, what did you do? You just left?"

"The next morning I drove past there at about 7am because I couldn't sleep. He was still there. I paged him a few more times. He didn't answer. At about 10, I rolled by there again. That time I saw Joe pulling away as I drove up the street. I was embarrassed. I kept thinking, what if he would've saw me, stalking this loser like a mad woman. Then I decided to write a note. I put the note on his car and I haven't looked back since."

"What did the note say?"

"It said, *Finance 101 – What you've paid for these past ten hours could have bought you a good tooth, you dumb bastard! KISS MY ASS you nasty TRICK!! If you try to call me, I'll kill you!*"

"Ooohhhh! No, you didn't!"

"Yes, I did."

"When was that?"

"About six months ago, and I haven't talked to him since. He sits outside my house, leaves me messages crying like a baby, sends me shit... I send it right back."

"I don't know if I'd do that."

"I don't want anything from him. Not his gifts, his apology, nothing."

"So, he never says anything when he's out in front of your house?"

"He's tried."

"What happened?"

"Nothing. I just ease my hand partially out of my pocket and let him get a glimpse of my buddy, Ms. Pearl Handle as she holds on to her pals Smith and Wesson."

"What?! What does he do?"

"What do you think? He gets his little string bean looking ass back in his car and sits there looking stupid. Once he held up a sign saying, *I'm sorry and I love you.*"

"No, he didn't."

"I gave his ass the finger with one hand and rubbed my pistol across my neck in a slicing motion with the other hand."

"Hah! Hah! Hah! You are nuts!"

"Yep, I sure am. That's exactly how he looked at me too. Like I was nuts. That's what I want him to know, I'm nuts."

"Fool. Fool. Fool. You are a fool, girl!"

"That's right. Whatever. Anyway, so are you going to be there awhile?"

"Yes, nut. I'll be here. Are you coming by?"

"I'm going to stop by for a minute. I just left Carmen's. She was pretty bombed out. They're going to start the foreclosure process in less than two weeks. Soon it'll be too late for her to save the house."

"How was she taking it?"

"She was trying to hold it together, but I could tell she was really down. I'm thinking we could just give her the check on tomorrow and call it a Christmas/Wedding gift. I know we initially said wedding gift, but that's a whole week away. That's a little too close for comfort… at least for me. I can't wait to see her face tomorrow. I should take a picture of her expression when she sees the check. I could take it to Walgreen's and have copies made to give to all of the ladies as Christmas gifts so that they can see just how much their selflessness and their sharing meant to her, her kids and basically everyone that knows her.

Miss Cool won't be able to hold back all that emotion. She's going to be ecstatic. She doesn't have a clue. I can't believe not one of the ladies let the cat out of the bag..."

"Sharon, Leah didn't call you?"

"Who?"

"Leah. Didn't she call you about the money?"

"No. Oh, shit. You gave her the check? I'm getting off at the exit by your house right now. Oh well, I guess I'll head across town to the other end of the city to her place. I don't feel like making this drive but my girl needs that check, so what the hell. Do you know if she's at home now?"

"Sharon, Leah was supposed to call you. After the meeting, it seems everybody got on the phone and discussed the whole thing. They voted. The result was, 'no'. Only two 'yes' votes were counted. Well, three if you include you."

"What did you say?"

"They voted 'no' to giving Carmen the money."

"You have got to be joking."

"No, Sharon, I'm sorry."

"You damn right about that! Sorry as hell! What type of fucking fair-weather friends are these?! When she was doing well and kicking ass, everybody was holding on to her coattail... Now, these phony... shit!"

Sharon grabbed the leather-covered steering wheel with both hands and turned it as hard as she could. Her tires squealed as she made a u-turn in the middle of the busy street. The driver of the U-Haul truck behind her wasn't happy. He whipped his truck beside her, stuck his hand out of the window and his lone middle finger saluted Sharon and her driving.

Seeing that, Sharon let down her window, raised her upper body out through the opening and yelled, "Fuck you, too!"

Once she was safely in her seat with the window up, she could hear Emily's voice coming through the phone.

"Sharon. Shar-ron! Sharon!"

Sharon rolled her eyes at the phone, then reached over and flipped the top cover down as hard as she could.

"Kiss my ass!"

22

Aces Wild

"Hello."

"Hello. Is this Trenton Art and Accents?"

"Uh, I guess it is." Carmen smiled.

"Well, this is Big Daddy and I need something beautiful in my life. I'd like that precious piece, *Carmen the Queen*. Can I get that piece?"

"I don't know, Sir. I do believe someone has already placed a deposit on that one."

"But you don't understand. That one was created for me. It's the only piece that will do for me. You'll have to get it back."

"Well, Sir, if you felt that way, you should have made a serious offer a long time ago."

"I'll pay any price. Take my house, my boat, my cars, my jewelry, anything…"

"Your wife?"

"Her too." Ace laughed. "That would help me out a lot."

"Yeah, right. What's up with you, Big Daddy?"

"You."

"That's what your mouth says."

"No, trust me, that's not the only thing that says so."

"Is that right?"

"Yeah. What's going on Mama? You okay? Everything alright?"

"I'm okay. What about you?"

"Missing you, that's all."

"I don't know... my caller ID keeps saying your lying."

"My caller ID says you're the one on some bulljive. You get you a little man and just kick ole Ace to the curb. He'll never love you like I love you, baby. You'd better keep things in their proper perspective. Ace knew you when you didn't even know yourself. If you try to fit that dude into my slot, he'll be found floating. I'm telling you now, you'd better let him know your heart belongs to Big Daddy. You hear me? Now come on over here and let Big Daddy show you some love."

Carmen sat smiling as she listened. Then instinctively she responded in a smooth, silky manner.

"Now, you know if Mama comes all the way out there, Big Daddy had better treat her right."

"Ohhhh, Big Daddy's gonna treat you right, all right. I miss you. I've got some new fantasies I'd like you to help me with. You should see what I've written lately. I've been dreaming about you. I want to see you. I need to see you. Moby has missed you, too. He can hear you. He's stretching out looking for you. Here say something to him."

"No, Ace. I don't have anything to say to Moby. I'm getting married in about a week and I don't think my husband would appreciate that."

"This doesn't have anything to do with him. Like you always say, this is between you and Moby."

"That's what I used to say."

"Oh, so you're going to treat Moby like that? That's messed up. Moby has never wronged you in any way. No matter where he is or who he's with, he's always thinking about you, wanting you, loving you. Now, you're going to act funny with him? I don't believe you. Come on, Carmen, don't do that. That's not right. You know that's not right."

"So, I should just say forget it, huh? Just act as if my fiancé doesn't exist? That's the thing to do? And that's what you would want your wife to do? Have lunch with somebody's Moby?"

"Come on, Carmen. You know we are way past that. I love you. I miss you. This is Ace you're talking to. Plus, you're not a wife yet. I really need to talk to you..."

"What time, Ace?" Carmen asked with a hint of irritation in her voice. "I hope you know that I'm not going to do anything with you. I can't. I just ..."

"Okay, woman. Whatever. Just come and see me."

"And I can't stay long, I've got some last minute gifts to pick up."

"See you at about four? I love you."

"Uhh, huh. Love you, too, Ace."

****

"It's been too long. I missed you." Ace managed to squeeze the words out as he hugged Carmen as tight as he could.

"I missed you, too, Ace," Carmen mumbled as she attempted to prevent her honey-colored lipstick from staining his off-white sweater. Marcus, Marcus, Marcus she reminded herself as she felt her body becoming lighter and lighter in the comfort of Ace's arms.

"Man, I missed you Carmen."

Ace separated himself. He stood holding Carmen's shoulders in his hands.

"What am I going to do with you?" He asked.

Carmen smiled. She loved Ace. She wished she didn't. He was so fine. He was a player. He was a sweetheart. He was a rat. He was loving. He was selfish. He was all of the things she dreamed of in a man and everything she'd sworn she would never accept in a man.

Ace knew exactly how she felt. He felt the same way about her.

"So, now what's this I hear?" Ace asked as he helped her with her coat.

"Well..."

"No, no, no, start at the beginning. When, who, how? Where did this come from all of a sudden?"

He sat Carmen on the couch, fluffed a pillow for her back, gently slid her boots off and placed her feet on the soft leather ottoman as he rambled the questions off.

"Start at the beginning? Well..." Carmen took a deep breath. "We met a few years back. I met him through Emily. He came by my shop a few times to bring food I'd ordered from Emily's restaurant..."

"Not that beginning," Ace interrupted. "The beginning of this marriage stuff. How did that come about? I don't want to hear all that other mess."

Carmen watched Ace as he placed a tea bag in the cup

she'd bought him years ago to celebrate the first poem he'd gotten published. How rude of him to ask something then pick and choose which answer he'd be willing to accept. But, that was Ace.

"Still two, right?" Ace smiled.

"Of course." Carmen replied.

"Well, I wasn't sure. Seems like a lot of things have changed. I just wanted to be sure."

Ace added two spoons of sugar and held the silver tray towards Carmen.

"Some things never change," Carmen replied as she took a sip of the tea.

"Thanks."

"No problem. Are you okay? You need anything else?"

Ace placed the tray on the floor and leaned back resting his neck on the arm of the couch at the end opposite Carmen. One leg was slightly bent, resting against the back of the couch, the other seemed to stretch far across the seat of the couch leaving a sinking valley which led right to the middle of his... person.

"Well..."

Again Carmen took a deep breath.

"I don't know, Ace. He just fits me."

"How so?"

Ace lifted up momentarily and pulled the sweater up and over his head. Then off of his perfectly piled, strong brown arms.

Carmen turned her head and took another deep breath then continued.

"He's settled. He helps around the house a lot. He

ummm..."

She could feel Ace staring at her. She took another sip of tea. It was too hot to just drink straight down.

"Wwwww. Wwwwww."

Carmen blew the tea to cool it down. She was hot. Ace was sooo cool. She took a gulp.

"Anyway, he, uh..."

"Talk to me, Carmen. I just want what's best for you. I love you... I want you to be okay."

Carmen turned to look at him. His eyes were red and filled with water. Half of his chin and one cheek was resting in the palm of his hand.

"Wwwwww. Wwwwww."

Carmen took another big gulp.

"Is he good to you?"

"Yeah. Yeah, he is."

"So, what is it. Carmen? You don't want to talk about it? This is very hard for me, listening to you talk about marrying somebody. I'm just asking you to help me deal with this. Help me to understand, to know that you'll be okay."

"I'll be alright." Carmen said softly as she raised the cup and took another big gulp.

"Do you love him?"

Carmen lifted the cup.

"Wwwww. Wwwwww."

She raised the cup to take another gulp.

"Wwwww. Wwwww."

She sipped. Empty. Nothing there.

"Ww..." She almost blew into the empty cup again.

"Come here, Carmen."

Ace was amazing. He always did this. He spoke in his regular tone as if he had nothing unacceptable on his mind, as if everything was in the name of friendship.

Carmen couldn't resist. She laid still in his valley.

"So, now, what made you want to marry this guy?"

"He's available."

"He's available?"

"Yep. He's there when I need him. He helps me a lot around the house."

"Like?"

"Like, fixing things, putting things together…you know, he's very handy with fixing things… and he's there. I can find him anytime I need him. There's somebody to handle the manly things. I get tired of being the man and the woman, all the time. Tired of making all the decisions alone."

"You are never alone. If you need somebody, call me. You don't need him for that."

"But don't you think I deserve a man of my own? Don't you think I'm worthy of that?"

"Yes, I do. Just tell me this, do you love him?"

"I'd say I must. I'm doing something I never thought I'd do again. I know he loves me."

"What does he do for a living?"

"Well, he sort of works with construction."

"Sort of? What does that mean?"

"He fixes things and put things together."

"What things?"

"All types of things."

"So, basically, he's a handyman."

"I guess you could say that."

"Okay. I don't have a problem with that. Not at all. As long as he earns a living and can take care of you and the kids. Now, tell me again... How do you know that you love him?"

"He's available."

"So just because he doesn't happen to have any odd jobs to do right now?"

"No. He helps me."

"How?"

"With the house. With everything. He can fix almost anything."

"He's a handyman, Carmen! He's supposed to fix shit. Just like the comedian you dated because he was funny and the actor because he was emotional and the ball player because he was athletic... Come on, Carmen. That's no reason to marry somebody, and you haven't said once that you really love him. That he truly makes you happy."

"Ace, you don't want me to be with anyone." Carmen tried to get up. Ace pulled her back to him.

Carmen continued.

"You have negative things to say about any guy I mention."

"That's because I think you deserve the best. If a guy can't love you more or treat you better than me, then you don't need him and I'm not going to sit idly by and watch you screw yourself."

"Let's not talk about this anymore."

Carmen's lips were as tight as if they'd been vacuum

sealed.

Carmen and Ace were silent for a couple of minutes.

"Carmen? Do I love you?"

"Yes."

"Do you love me?"

"Yes Ace, I do."

"I know you do. That's all I'm trying to say, that's what it should feel like. Listen. Do you remember that poem I wrote for you years ago? The first poem in the first book I ever got published?"

Carmen knew the exact piece Ace was referring to. It was the poem that held her bound to him. Whenever she'd question her relationship with him she'd remember that poem and it would erase all faults and displeasures.

Carmen lay motionless in his valley again. She wished for a cup of tea to blow to cool herself off.

"Lift up for a minute."

Ace sat up. He lifted a sort of large wrapped package from behind the couch.

"Merry Christmas. Just in case I couldn't talk you out of it, I thought I'd give you something to let you know that I will always be here for you. Go ahead and open it."

It was a piece by Holyfield entitled, The Poet. Just like the poem Ace had written for her.

"When I saw it I knew I had to have it." Ace said.

Carmen was quiet for a moment. She couldn't believe how Holyfield, the artist had managed to capture the essence of Ace's poem and the feel of she and Ace's relationship during it's early stages. Ace could have easily lied and said he commissioned the guy to paint the picture and Carmen would have believed it. That's just how accurate it was.

"Aw, Ace. You should have told me you wanted to exchange gifts. I didn't know. I didn't get you anything."

Carmen felt bad. In all the years she'd known Ace, they'd never exchanged gifts for holidays. They believed the gifts they gave each other were much more special than anything that could be given on command or purchased at a store. At least that's the way Ace had explained it years ago. Carmen had simply agreed.

"Don't worry about it, Carmen. I don't need a store bought gift. I do know of something that you could give me."

"What's that, Mr. Hot Daddy?"

Ace stared into Carmen's eyes.

"You can promise me that we can keep this. This is special. I need you. Promise me we can keep this, forever."

Carmen threw her head back and looked at the ceiling.

"Wwwwwww."

She reached her arms around him and gave him the hug he'd hope for when she'd entered the room.

"Promise," she whispered.

Ace lifted her into the air and somehow worked his way onto the couch. This time they lay still, his entire body on the couch and her on the mountain top of his manhood.

Carmen thought about how it was that Ace always knew what to say and when to say it. He always made her feel valued and special.

She thought about Marcus and the house and the lost money. She wondered why she didn't just ask Ace for it. He loved her. He wanted her to be happy. Surely he could afford to loan her the money. Actually, he could afford to give her the money, but she wouldn't want him to think she was needing his money, or wanting his money. If Ace knew she was in trouble he would jump at the chance to help her. At least that's what she told herself.

"Ace."

"Yeah, Baby?"

"I have a confession to make."

"What is it?" Ace asked as he turned and kissed Carmen on her forehead.

"Well, earlier today when I said I was doing okay, I lied."

Ace was silent.

"Actually, I'm in a little trouble."

Ace lay still.

"I invested in a business deal that went sour. Plus, the IRS is coming after me. Well, the bottom line is, I'm going to lose my house if I don't come up with fourteen thousand dollars within the next ten days. I don't have any way to come up with the money. If you could just loan me the money, I will definitely get it back to you."

Carmen felt weird. This was the first time she'd ever asked Ace for money. She lifted up on her arms. Ace was still and his eyes were closed.

"Ace. Ace." She nudged him. "Ace, did you hear me?"

"Yes," he said groggily.

"I could get the money back to you by May 1st. Ace are you listening?"

"Man, Carmen. I wish you would have told me sooner.

I just promised my wife's mother fifty thousand to get new landscaping at her summer home."

"Oh, are you two friends now?"

"No." Ace responded slowly. "I don't like her. My wife kept bugging me, so I said okay."

What is all this my wife shit? Carmen thought to herself. She is his wife, but he's never referred to her as "wife."

"So when do you have to give her the money? By the time the weather will permit landscaping to be done, I will have given the money back."

Ace was silent.

"Ace. Ace. Are you listening, Ace."

"Shhh. Shhh. What time is it? Look over there on that table."

"Seven."

"Oh, shit." Ace sat up slowly and started putting his clothes on. "The elevator is coming up. That must be Suzy. I didn't know it was this late. I was supposed to take her shopping. Damn."

"Lock the door!" Carmen said quickly.

Ace moved slowly.

"She won't come in here. I've got to get out of here. Do me a favor, Carmen. When you leave, go down the backstairs. I'm going to meet them out there in the front office. Just close the door behind you."

Ace kissed her on her lips. "Call me later, okay?"

"Yeah."

"Make sure, Carmen. Love you."

Ace grabbed his jacket and rushed out the door.

"Oh, Merry Christmas, Baby. Buy the kids something nice from me." He tossed some crumbled up bills towards a nearby chair. Then, his other hand tossed a stack of bills he'd found in another pocket. "That's all I've got on me."

With that, he ducked his head back out of the door and was gone.

One thousand, two hundred and twelve dollars it added up to be.

A few minutes later, Carmen exited through the door leading to the back stairs. She discovered there actually weren't any back stairs. The door Ace had directed her to, lead to the fire escape. The stairs were already lowered but they were covered with snow and ice. It was a dangerous situation. Carmen twisted the knob on the door hoping to go back into the office but the door had locked behind her.

"I don't believe this damn, Ace. Motherfucker!"

Carmen stood looking down the stairs wondering how she could possibly make it down in her 3" high-heeled boots.

"Motherfucking, Ace!" She yelled as she slowly made her way down the steps and into the dark alley.

She only fell twice.

Once when she lost her footing on the curb she couldn't see due to the snow, and another time when the wind caught hold of that picture she was carrying. Just like a kite, the wind lifted her, pulled her right up out of the snow like she could fly. Then, just as quick as it had snatched her up, it dropped her, ass first into the dirty slush puddle in the center of the end of the alley.

Carmen sat there, cold, wet and frustrated. Mud and dirt everywhere. Her snakeskin boots, her good coat; all covered in mud. There were even specks on her face. But not the picture. There wasn't one speck of mud on that picture. Just like Ace, the picture had made it through the ordeal without a blemish. Thanks to Carmen. She sat there in the mud, arms above her head, gripping the picture, sacrificing anything and everything possible to keep Ace and his gift spot free.

23

Merry X-Mas

"Sorry about this everybody. What time is it now?"

"Nine-thirty." Candice, Carmen's sister, rolled her eyes and took a deep breath as she turned to answer Carmen.

"I don't know where Tyrone is. He was only supposed to take them for a couple of hours. He said they were going to his parents house," Carmen rambled apologetically.

"Did you call over there?" Mrs. Trenton asked.

"I called about eight hours ago, right after they left. They forgot his parents' gifts.

I called to find out if he'd come back and get them or if he needed me to drop them off. I didn't want the kids over there empty handed. I called his cell number, his mama's house and his house."

"Did you ask his mother to have him call you?" Mrs. Trenton asked.

"Of course."

"And he hasn't called yet?" Mrs. Trenton asked as if she didn't already know the answer.

"No. He hasn't called and he isn't answering his phone. I'm thinking something may have happened. Maybe I should call the police."

"I don't know, Carmen. Maybe you should. This isn't like Tyrone. He knows we always celebrate Christmas together. He wouldn't normally take the kids and stay gone all day like this, especially on Christmas Day!" Mrs. Trenton sounded irritated.

"You know what? You all can go ahead and open your presents. You don't have to keep waiting for them." Carmen waved her hand in the air.

"No! The kids will be really disappointed if we open the gifts without them. It's a family tradition. Tyson and Tysa pass out the gifts and we all open our gifts in the presence of one another. We take pictures..."

Mrs. Trenton's voice was higher than normal.

She continued, "Tysa helps me fold the wrapping paper that's salvageable. Tyson gets the big, black Hefty bag and goes around collecting torn paper, ugly paper and empty boxes!"

Candice interrupted. "Actually, I don't think Tyson would mind if someone else handled that part of the tradition."

"The kids and I are going to have to get going." Carla sighed. "I have to take them over to their other folks house. They're probably in bed by now but we'd better stop by anyway or my name will be mud, if it isn't already. Get your coats kids."

'Well, I really don't know what to say." Carmen looked tired. "Merry Christmas, y'all. Randy and Raynard get under that tree and get your presents. Take them with you. I don't know what in the hell is up with Tyrone."

"No!" Mrs. Trenton jumped right. "Leave the presents! We are going to do this the way we always do it. If not today, we'll do it tomorrow."

Mrs. Trenton was filled with mixed emotions. She loved Tyrone. She'd known him almost twenty years. She'd watched him grow into a fine young man. But this was unacceptable.

"It isn't those kids fault that their daddy is being a butthole! Put that back Raynard. Come from under that tree, Randy. Stop looking. Leave it alone. Candice, come on in this kitchen and help me put this food up."

As she headed towards the kitchen she saw that Carmen was on the phone. She wished she could take away the pain. She could see it in Carmen's face. She could feel it. Her heart was pounding. She was getting too old for all this drama. She wanted to tell Carmen it was okay, but she knew that it really wasn't. She had hoped Tyrone was one of the other kind. The kind that did their share of wrong but ultimately matured and grew out of their selfish ways. But she was sure, especially now, Tyrone was one of the others. The kind that grew progressively worse. The kind that mistook kindness for weakness. The kind that believed they had the power... their women wouldn't leave them because they couldn't leave them. Mrs. Trenton knew that for Carmen, the worse was yet to come. She would have to stand up and fight. There would have to be a showdown and Carmen would have to hold her own. No one could do it for her. The reality lay heavy on her heart. The inevitable pissed her off! Why couldn't Tyrone be one of the others?

Mrs. Trenton breathed deeply as she grumbled loudly from the kitchen.

"We'll be back tomorrow Carmen," she said.

Carmen slammed the phone down. "This fool has lost his mind."

"No answer?" Carla asked.

Carmen didn't say a word. She exhaled a breath that hit the room like an Ali jab.

"What time is it? Ten?"

"No, Carla. Its 10:12." Mrs. Trenton responded sharply.

"Wake up your father, Candice. Let's go on home. Carmen, you call me when they get here to let me know that the kids are alright."

"Call me too, Carmen. I'm gonna go ahead and stop by their grandparents so they can drop off their gifts before the stroke of midnight. Legally, it's still Christmas. I guess I'm covered, huh?"

Carla could feel Carmen's heat. She tried to joke and make light of the situation. She loved her sister and didn't want to have to get up in the middle of the night, scrape her money together and go bail Carmen out of jail.

"I'll be at home after that. Be sure to call me, okay?"

Carla walked towards the door. "Actually, the kids will probably love this. Two full days of Santa."

Mrs. Trenton on the other hand, was pissed. She had no energy for the Cosby Show role playing bullshit.

"My blood pressure is probably through the ceiling. Don't worry, Carmen. They'll be okay. But you need to tell Tyrone about himself."

Mrs. Trenton held her head high and proud as she exited through the front door.

"Let him know…"

Carmen didn't say a word.

"This is ridiculous! He thinks he can just do whatever he

wants, whenever he wants, however he wants."

Mrs. Trenton continued as Mr. Trenton shut her car door. Carmen could still hear her snapping.

"I wouldn't have this mess! She is going to have to get him straight. He wouldn't see mine if he couldn't respect my wishes."

She continued talking as the car pulled off. Carmen stood in the doorway watching. She no longer could hear her mother's voice but she could still see her lips moving.

"Bye, Sis. Merry Christmas. Don't worry about it. Call me if you need me. I'll be at home. Tell my niece and nephew to call me when they get in."

"Bye, Ben."

Benjamin Trenton was Carmen's brother's real name. Carmen and her sister's renamed him Benjamin Franklin because of his stoic demeanor. He was just like their dad, who's only parting words had been the baritone, "Turkey's in the cooler" and "Take care, baby."

Carmen locked the door, grabbed the phone and plopped down on the sofa.

"Turkey's in the cooler?"

Carmen recalled her father's voice. She jumped up, grabbed her coat and headed to the garage. *Turkey in the cooler...* Translation, there wasn't enough room in the fridge, so I sat your turkey in the garage. The turkey you plan to eat tomorrow. In the garage. The garage with squirrels, spiders and God only knows what else. Carmen's dad was born in Mississippi. He considered it a privilege when opportunities arose where he could use his southern nostalgic survival antics.

He knew Carmen didn't like it but so what? She should. Sort of like her mother giving the kids juice from the collard greens when they were only two months old, and her sister continually giving Tysa candy, though Tysa was only four years old and already had two cavities. Family ties. Tattered old family ties that Carmen wouldn't trade for the world.

Carmen slammed the door shut with her butt. The Chicago Hawk was out and it was obvious he was more angry than she. The thin foil pan was bending. It wasn't sturdy enough to hold the turkey and dressing. At least not through this type of movement. The music was on. The TV was on. The dishwasher was grinding. The bell was ringing. The bell was ringing! Carmen quickly plopped the pan on the counter and rushed to the door.

"Hi, ma. Is everybody gone?" Tyson asked nervously.

"Are you all okay? Where is Tyrone?"

Carmen was pushing past the kids when she heard a loud thump. She knew instantly it was the turkey. She started to turn around, then opted to deal with Tyrone first. That is, until she heard the sound of Tyrone's engine fading in the distance.

"Sorry, ma." Tyson said. "We tried to get here."

Carmen was silent as she repeatedly dialed Tyrone's cell phone number.

"Tyrese got a lot of presents, ma! My dad got him a phone like yours. He bought him a two-way pager. It's sweet! He got a CD player. It's kinda of like yours but it's new and it's sweet. Plus ma, he got a real leather case for his. It's ost-ik skin."

"How do you know, Tysa?" Carmen asked as she reminded herself that it was not proper to curse in front of children and even less acceptable to curse them out!

Tysa was four going on forty. Carmen wished for a moment that Tyson had gone downstairs somewhere so that she could tell this little wench exactly where to put her nice, great dad. And the word is ostrich, smart-ass.

"He did, ma. He got a lot of stuff." Tyson's eyes, nose and mouth widened as excitement oozed from every pore of his body. "He got a flat-screen TV for his bedroom, and he still has the other TV he got last year. You know those earrings you have? The diamond ones. He got some but his are huge!"

Carmen was becoming more and more irritated by the excitement she could hear in Tyson's voice. She dreaded the time her children had to spend in that world. The world of things. Where the sole concern was who had, and who could get the biggest and best of everything. She could remember Tyrese at five years old, taunting her when he got his first diamond earring.

"You don't have any diamond earrings and you are a grown lady. I'm only five and I've got better stuff than you. That's why you make me take my earring out when I come to your house. You just jealous because you don't have enough money and my dad won't buy you any."

Carmen's response had only been a cool, calm, "Is that what someone told you, sweetie? Always remember, Ms. Carmen always gets what she wants to get, not what small minds think she should have."

That night Carmen had cried. She realized Tyrese was only a small child, but that didn't remove the fact that he was repeatedly disrespecting her in his own childish way. A way taught to him by his mama, a modern day slave, frequently sold to the highest bidder. She had married five times with not one of them lasting for more than one year. She was a cute woman but she lacked self-esteem. Not low self-esteem, no self-esteem. She was a slave for sure. A slave with shiny gold shoe-shackles. She was a professional. She spent her every waking moment searching for the wizard. She'd camelion-ized herself so many times that she was left without the slightest clue as to who she was. Contrary to what Tyrone would have everyone believe, Carmen did not hate the woman. She only hated the things she stood for. She hated the influence her interactions, ignorance and lack of self-love would have on Tyson, Tysa and even Carmen herself. The woman had wronged Carmen several times. Nevertheless, Carmen couldn't hate her. She understood her. Thanks to Spring. If anything, Carmen pitied her. She pitied Tyrese, too.

Tyson caught his breath and continued.

"He got three Coogie sweaters, four FUBU outfits, a black Iceberg outfit like the blue one he got last month. He got a bunch of CD's... Ludacris, Ja-Rule, Jay-Z, Lil Kim, Trina... I can't even remember all of them. He got everybody, ma and he got the unedited versions! My dad said he would have got them for me too, but you said he couldn't. Man, Ma."

"That's right. You don't need to listen to that ghetto bull all day, everyday."

"But what's the difference? I hear it on the radio all the time. Plus, I hear language worse than that at school everyday. I'm not a baby, ma. I can't believe you a hater, like my dad said."

Tyson leaned over and reached for the phone.

Carmen's eyes were fixed on him as she sat in silence.

"Can I call grandma?"

"See that? See how you still have to ask to use the phone?" Carmen spoke slowly.

Tyson looked confused.

"When you can grab the phone confidently and just call who you want and say what you want because you pay your own damn bills in your own damn house, then you can listen to all the garbage you want. And you can bling-bling, ching-ching or whatever else you want. But until then, this is my house. I'm the parent and I..."

"... make the rules." Tyson said in unison with Carmen.

Carmen tossed him an evil eye.

Tyson patted her knee slowly.

"I know, ma," he said with a smirk on his face.

Carmen raised her eyebrows and rolled her eyes.

"I know you know. I'm wondering why you're playing with me. I'm not in the mood, Tyson."

"Sorry, ma."

"Did you and your dad forget your family was waiting here for you and Tysa?"

"I kept telling him, ma. And Tysa even almost got a whipping."

"A whipping for what?"

"She wanted to come home and she was crying and stuff. Plus, she didn't want to play with the kids. She kept trying to stay with my dad. She was crying because Tyrese's uncle picked her up and made her kiss him."

"What did your dad say?"

"What? About the kiss?"

"Yeah."

"He wasn't there then, I think."

"What do you mean, you think? Where were you? Why weren't you watching her?"

"She was with Liz, ma, my brother's mother." Tyson added sarcastically.

"I don't care if it was your brother's mother, your brother or your brother's father for that matter. You are supposed to watch her and protect her."

"My brother's father?" Tyson looked confused.

"That's right and you be careful how you handle her yourself, too. You can look at me like I'm crazy if you want to, but if anything happens to her, we'll see what crazy really looks like."

****

Carmen lie in bed, eyes swollen from the salt of her midnight tears. The Bible says, *Weeping may endure for a night, but joy comes in the morning.* What morning, Carmen wondered. Was that a riddle of some sort? Daybreak had come a couple of hours ago. Carmen was sure of that fact. She had waited patiently for it. Watching the clock. Counting the hours, minutes and seconds. Depending on God's promise. Believing in God's words. Yet, she lay there wishing someone would find her joy and send it home. She was waiting with hopeful anticipation. She would welcome joy with open arms, but there was no sign of it.

What about Marcus? She hadn't even considered

phoning Marcus, not once through the whole ordeal. Surely Marcus was busy running his and everyone else's errands. Or maybe he was still comforting his mom. He had opted to spend Christmas with his mother so that she wouldn't be lonely. Carmen had suggested that he bring his mom to her house for the day but his mom had refused, saying she wanted to be at her own home doing what she does and has done for the better part of sixty-five years. She had told Marcus that she'd understand if he wanted to go and do new things with his new family... he shouldn't worry about her, she'd be okay, at home all by herself on Christmas Day. Then when Carmen had attempted to discuss it, Marcus had asked her to be understanding. She would have him 365 days a year for the rest of their lives, the least she could do was share him with his mom for a few of those days. Carmen had conceded. Though she felt there was a winnable argument hidden just beneath the surface of it all, she didn't have the strength to fight.

As she thought about Marcus, she felt herself getting depressed again, she reminded herself of the reason for the season. Who was she to be pissed at life and life's trials and tribulations?

When she'd felt similar to this some years ago, Rita had suggested they become prayer partners and they spoke each and every morning via phone. Rita had taught her an exercise that was a big help in preparing her mind to deal with the likes of the good-ole-boys at her previous job.

Maybe. Who knows?...

She closed her eyes.

"Peace be still," she repeated slowly as she began

meditation efforts.

She was careful to breathe deeply just as Rita had taught her.

"Peace be still. Peace be still..."

Ring, ring, ring.

Carmen reluctantly reached over to answer the phone. She had hoped Tyson or even Tysa would answer it, but apparently they were still sleeping.

"Hello."

"Tell the kids to get ready. I'll be there to get them in about thirty minutes."

"No, I don't think so."

"I'm taking them to my mother's."

"No, that can't happen."

"I can't take them to my mother's?"

"Tyrone, didn't I ask you not to take my kids out to Tyrese's house?"

"Look, you don't tell me what to do with my kids."

"But I've explained to you and I've asked you politely..."

"Explained what? I'm not dealing with your childish jealous bullshit. I'm a grown ass man. You can't raise me. I keep telling you that! I do what the hell I want to do and you are not going to dictate to me what I can or can not do with my own children... where I can or can't take them."

"Tyrone, I'm not trying to argue with you. I am just asking you to be considerate and respectful of my wishes."

"Like I said, you're not going to tell me what to do."

"Tyrone, why do you have to be such an asshole about

everything? All I ask is that you don't take my kids to that house. My kids don't have to go to that house."

"You sound stupid. Their brother lives in that house!"

"So what? They can see their brother at your house or your mother's house. They don't have to go there. How fair is it for you to take my kids to her house on the holiday? You take my kids and make them participate in that family's celebration while their own family waits all day for them to come back home."

"I don't want to hear this stupid shit! Have my kids ready in half an hour."

"They have something else to do."

"You are one ignorant motherfucker! You need help. I've never met a dumbass motherfucker as stupid as you. Just because you are childish, crazy and jealous, you think I'm supposed to kiss your ass? Well, that's not gonna happen! You are crazy and you need to have yourself checked."

"Don't talk to me like that!"

"You don't tell me how to fucking talk to you!"

"Why do I have to be stupid, dumb and crazy because I ask you to treat me decently?"

"I'm not treating you like shit! I'm not thinking about your stupid ass!"

"I know, Tyrone. You only think of yourself. That's why you will never be happy and you will never have anything."

"Fuck you, you broke bitch… with your lazy, trifling ass! Get a fucking real job! That's why you have to move! With your broke ass. You ignorant bitch!"

Carmen was silent.

She didn't know what to say, how to respond. Never had

she felt such pain.

Tyrone's words dug deep into her flesh. She could feel his hatred. Nothing he'd ever done compared to this moment. She'd worked at least two jobs consistently for the past ten years to support herself, Tyson and now Tysa. She'd handled childbirth expenses, karate classes and everything in between. It was Carmen who had stayed up late nights through the chronic ear infections and fevers, not Tyrone. Yet, he was calling her lazy?! The one thing no one could call Carmen Trenton was lazy. Carmen was a workaholic, always pushing herself to do more. How dare Tyrone be so cruel and vicious! There was a time when she would have died for Tyrone. She thought he could do no wrong. Now, he made her sick to the stomach. His blatant disregard for her feelings made him look as ugly as anything she'd ever seen. She had never required anything but love from his ungrateful ass. She now realized, she had never even demanded his respect.

Tyrone continued.

"You think you can run everything! I don't give a shit about..."

"Tyrone."

Carmen interrupted his ranting and raving.

"Chew my cherry, you ignorant bastard!"

"Okay, I don't have a problem with that. Bring it to me and I will."

Realizing her effort to piss Tyrone off was actually turning him on, Carmen slammed down the phone as hard as she could.

"I don't have to deal with his bullshit!!"

24

Good Morning Diary

December 29th –

Today is a new day. I am going to try to embrace it as such. It seems like to hard a task for me right now. My whole world is wobbly.

I've got to deal with the ladies today. Sharon doesn't know that I know about the vote. Emily mentioned it because she was sure Sharon had told me. But she was wrong. I haven't discussed it with anyone. I have too much drama right now. I don't have a drop of energy to spare. I'm drained. It seems as though negativity has me like quick sand… sucking me in, pulling me down rapidly, smoothly.

Sharon called me earlier and suggested we go to a spa. She said she needed to relax. I know she just wants to keep me from the meeting. She thinks she has to protect me. I'm really okay with the whole thing. It is the group's money not mine. They are not required to loan it to me. I can't get mad about it. I must say, I'm not too happy about them discussing my business and passing judgement on me and my life. I never asked for their help nor their comments and interference.

In a way, I guess the reality is a bit disturbing. There are only a couple of people on this earth who would sacrifice something for me. The sad balance of it is that those who would help me, can't help me and those who can, won't. That's the irony of life, I guess.

I think I'm going to skip the spa and attend the meeting instead. I need to face the music. I'll just keep quiet and listen today. I think there are some things I haven't been hearing. I may even take some notes. I need to have a reminder of what's real. I've learned a lot these past few weeks.

Only three "yes" votes. Huh. Can you believe that? If it wasn't so real, I wouldn't believe it myself. I really don't want to but I need to.

Rita called me early this morning. She told me of how she'd gone before the church board on my behalf. She said it had been a difficult task but with God by her side, she'd been victorious. She'd convinced the church to allow me to start teaching my classes again. She never mentioned anything about the letter and she probably never will. She said they want me to start as soon as I can, after the wedding of course. But of course.

The Beautiful Ones.

Rita.

Tyrone.

Ace... and his wife.

And yes, even Marcus

*It feels lonely. I feel empty. But... I'm gonna wait here... right here in the thick of things... and listen. Listen for the sound of the birds. Watch the sun and the moon. Feel the pinch of the wind as it assures me that I **am not** dreaming.*

How I wish it was springtime...

25

Full Moon

You could hear the chattering from the street. Laughter bounced playfully off the cars and SUV's that lined the driveway. The aura from the inside of Emily's newly built suburban mini-mansion lit up the quiet neighborhood like a gorgeous, gigantic fireplace full of good, dry natural logs. The warmth emanating from the guts of it's existence. Yet, Carmen wasn't affected. As she and Sharon approached the door, the cold air seemed to form an impenetrable layer of frost around them that could extinguish a full-fledge forest fire, much less the heated souls of a dozen or so back-biting women. Carmen had hoped to be humble and to sort of exude a sense of peace and solace, but she hadn't been able to persuade the monkey of depression to disengage her and find a better back. It didn't help that she had spent the last twenty minutes listening to the ramblings of Jay-Z, and the growling of DMX. Carmen couldn't figure out if Sharon wanted her to _Get her mind right_, as Jay-Z had so eloquently suggested in his smooth-grooving misogynistic-lyric laced track or get frustrated while being enlightened by the too-hard-to-handle realities of DMX's soul growling declaration, _They don't know who we be._

As they waited to enter the house, Carmen silently sang

the song her mother used to sing when she was trying to determine appropriate disciplinary action for Carmen and her siblings wrongdoings – *"Yes, Jesus loves me... Yes, Jesus loves me... Yes, Jesus loves me, for the Bible tells me so. Jesus loves me, this I know, for the Bible tells me so..."*

Carmen breathed deeply. It was working. It was calming her spirit. The older she got, the more she understood her mother and the reasons she did the things she did. As children, Carmen, her sisters and her brothers thought their mother had a double. Their real mother was the nice one who played games, helped with arts and craft projects and fixed lunches. That other woman was some sort of sadist. They didn't have a clue as to where she came from or how she'd finagle her way into their home. Carmen almost laughed out loud as she pictured the nonchalant facial expression her mother wore as she sang her calming song. She wished she had a mirror now, she was sure she was wearing the Jesus loves me face that used to belong to her mother. The infamous rumor - if you want to know what a girl will be like as a woman, look at her mother – was proving to be more fact than fiction.

"Hey y'all, just in time. We thought we were going to have to start without you. Get on in here, give me those coats and grab a seat."

Emily moved quickly. Within moments she was back at the doorway of the huge recreation room.

"Okay ladies, today we're going to talk about something that I am very familiar with, and that is, success! I signed up for this topic because I felt I had a lot of pointers I could share with all of you. I have been blessed to get very far in business. I started my first business at the young age of twenty. I didn't know what I was doing, all I knew is, if it could be done, I could do it. I believe you have to have a dream first. Without a dream and/or vision, you have nothing. No one can give you what it takes to be a successful entrepreneur. In order to achieve greatness, you must be somewhat ignorant to the rules of society. Society will tell you it ain't possible – it ain't done that way – it ain't supposed to be like that, but you have to have a dream and relentlessly pursue your dream. They told me the restaurant business didn't make money. They had all the statistics to support their gibberish. They said my chances of existing for more than a year were slim, according to history. But I knew I could cook my ass off and with mama Frison's secret family recipes as the anchor for my business, nothing was going to stop me. Now, I have five restaurants in three different cities!

Don't tell me what can or can not be done! I'm living proof! I ain't have shit ten years ago. I made so many mistakes during my early years of business. I was trying to do it the way others told me it was supposed to be done. Fancy look, fancy food, live jazz bands, reservations required... all that other crazy bulljive. I totally went against myself and my dream and that's why I kept having setbacks. When lack of finances forced me to open up a little hole in the wall soul kitchen, I was just trying to hold on. I just did what I personally knew how to do. I wasn't trying to get rich, I was trying to eat on a daily basis. I put all my effort into making that food as tasty as I could so that the people would come back regularly."

Emily grabbed the nearby notepad and began reading.

"Booker T. Washington said: *To be successful, grow to*

the point where one completely forgets himself – that is, to lose himself in a great cause. That's exactly what I did and that's when it happened for me. Folks in the ghetto spread the word and next thing I knew I couldn't cook enough food. Ain't nothing like word of mouth. I was forced to open my second place across town. I didn't put all that money into decorating and fancy fluff, like I had the other times. I made it decent and kept it clean. But I made sure the food was always fresh, hot and delicious.

So I guess I'm saying, follow your heart, concentrate on your passion and not the money, and work like a dog. It'll get hard but you've got to hold on!"

Emily was smiling. She always got excited when she spoke about business and cooking. That combination was her passion. She'd given her whole speech without ever pausing to catch her breath. She'd even added arm movement and animated motions, yet she stood energized, ready to continue if given the opportunity.

Emily continued. "If you commit yourself to your work, you will be just as successful. Maybe even more so."

Then Rita spoke.

"Well, that's true in anything you do. If you commit and apply yourself you'll achieve whatever you set out to do. In all areas of your life. I don't own a business but I feel I'm successful. I do volunteer work for the church and it's as rewarding for me as your business success is for you. I think it's important to stress that having lots of money and fine things aren't the only signs of success. Praise God. James Baldwin said – *American equation of success with the big times reveals an awful disrespect for human life and achievement. This equation has placed our youths among the most empty and bewildered.* So, I think it's all about what you want out of life and what you feel is God's purpose for your life. I like to think I'm pleasing God by trying to make a difference in lives. The thought of me pleasing God is what success looks and feels like to me. So again, I'd say it all depends."

"That's true but even the Bible says, *Man don't work, Man don't eat.* Now, that's what the Bible says, huh, not me. I think you've gotta be ready and willing to handle a few things. I think it's all about priorities and what's in your heart. Cause serving God is a great thing but I ain't never heard it said that praising God meant you had to be broke down, naked, hungry and homeless. You've got to make serving God a part of your business. God is the greatest entrepreneur of all times. You know what I mean?"

Emily looked side to side searching faces for signs of approval.

Everyone was busy trying to digest the fact that Rita could quote something other than the Bible. Carmen seemed to be in a daze. She was preoccupied with Rita's statement. It was the almost the exact statement, quote and all, that she'd used to help Rita make the transition from flamboyant hustler's queen to self-respecting Christian woman.

Emily's voice was filled with sarcasm as she continued.

"Now, I guess we can get to work. We're going to start with a few exercises that Carmen prepared. Following that we'll have discussion. Carmen."

Emily opened her arm out to the side as if introducing a

performer.

Carmen looked towards Emily. She was surprised. She had totally forgotten that she'd agreed to prepare one of her creative exercises.

"I don't have anything," she said somberly.

"It totally slipped my mind. Why don't we just open up the floor for discussion?"

"You forgot? How could you forget something like that? Especially on my presentation day."

Emily smiled but her seriousness was evident. She continued.

"I've got the one exercise you gave me a few weeks ago. I made copies of that. I guess we can at least do that one, then we'll open up for discussion."

Emily grabbed the stack of paper from the top of the mantel and began distributing them.

"Do you remember this exercise? And what you wanted us to do with it?"

Carmen stared at the paper.

"It's kind of self-explanatory," she said. She let out a deep sigh.

"The triangle represents your life. List the aspects of your life in order of importance, starting at the top of the pyramid with #1 being the most important and #7 being the least important. Under each number you should expound, using no more than four brief points to articulate your thoughts."

Carmen looked up from the paper and leaned back in her seat.

"So does everyone understand the assignment?" Emily

asked.

"No." Renee said abruptly. "Where do we get the categories? You know. The list?"

Everyone was silent waiting for Carmen to respond. She didn't.

"Carmen." Emily called.

She spoke a little loud assuming she needed to wake Carmen or bring her back from the twilight zone.

"What categories do you want us to use?" Renee asked. Carmen responded in a low tone.

"What do you mean?"

"I mean, how are we supposed to know which things to use? Are you talking business, personal, what?" Renee spurted.

Her patience with Carmen was growing thin. So what she didn't get the money. Get over it. Participate or don't participate but this crazy act is working my damn nerves.

"What – do – you – want – us – to – write?" Renee asked slowly as if talking to a visitor from another planet.

Carmen wasn't far enough removed from her experience with Jay-Z and DMX to allow Renee to screw with her today.

"Do you not understand what I mean when I say, list what's most important in *your* life? **In your life.** Do you need me to tell you what's most important in your life? I've got a hard enough time with my life, and now you want me to define yours?"

"All I asked, was for you to explain your little exercise. You ain't got to get all indignant with me."

Emily cut in.

"Well now we all know what to do."

Emily scrunched her forehead as she looked at the ladies as if to ask, *What in the hell is up with Carmen?*

"So, let's just get rolling. I have Carmen's. If you don't understand, you can use hers as an example. Pass this around."

Emily held the paper out towards Leah.

"No! Don't pass that around. The whole idea is for each person to pull from their inner-self. If you look at my categories, it'll give direction or influence and you'll think those are areas you should include. There are no right and wrong categories. You decide for yourself which areas of life are important to you."

Carmen reached for the paper.

Emily handed it to her.

"O-k-a-y." Emily conceded as she attempted to keep things moving.

The ladies busied themselves completing the assignment.

Meanwhile Carmen went into the kitchen and poured herself a drink. After about twenty minutes, once everyone stopped writing, they began the discussion.

Carmen explained the second half of the assignment.

"On the back of the paper you are supposed to fill in the other triangle with the things that you think represent success. If your pyramid doesn't match the pyramid of success on the back, then you need to work on some things in your life to ultimately make your life pyramid match your success pyramid."

That was all Carmen said for the remainder of the evening. She sat quietly taking notes as planned.

Most of the other ladies were quiet as well.

When it was time to leave, Rita courageously stepped into Carmen's personal space and she hugged her. Without mumbling a word, she hugged her.

Sharon could feel Carmen's emotions and she too hugged her. That was followed by a hug from each and every woman in the room. They hugged Carmen and each other. Finally when they'd exhausted themselves and their unspoken apologies were communicated, they'd closed the meeting in prayer led by an unexpected volunteer.

This was the first time they'd ever done this type of thing and of all people, Amy had suggested it.

As they filed out and headed to their respective homes, Carmen couldn't help but notice the moon – it was round, bright, full, and it was complete.

26

Love Is

Knock. Knock. Knock.

Carmen awoke to the sound of hard knocking which bordered banging. She reluctantly got out of bed and headed to the door.

Knock. Knock. Knock.

Knock. Knock. Knock. The sound got louder.

Carmen eased herself down until she was seated on the steps – halfway down.

Her face wore a smirk of sarcasm.

"Let's just see how long and how hard this fool is going to knock on my damn door."

Knock. Knock. Knock.

Knock. Knock. Knock.

The knocks kept coming. Maybe this was an emergency. Why else would someone be so persistent and so rude. Carmen gave in to her thoughts.

"Wait a minute!" She yelled. "Wait!"

She slowly opened the door.

"Yes?! What is it?"

"I'm sorry. I just need you to sign acknowledging that I completed your wash."

"What?"

"Your wash." The brown skin man stepped to the side. His words snugly wrapped in thick puffs of frosty smoke lingered lazily on top of the air making it difficult for Carmen to see.

"C4 Services?" Carmen managed to read the lettering on the van. "What is this?"

Carmen's face was covered in ugly curiosity. Her head was banging. She'd just managed to get to sleep at about 5am. Now here's this man talking about a wash and C4 and signing something...

"Marcus requested that we wash your vehicle this morning. I was done ten minutes ago. All I need is a signature from you and I'll be on my way."

The cold, irritated man stared at Carmen as he held the clipboard towards her. The sun offered a blinding ray to shed light on the situation. Her van sparkled like new capturing every fleck of light the sun charitably donated on the icy-cold winter morning.

"Oh. Wash. How'd you do that?" Carmen took the clipboard and signed her name next to the 'X' on the dotted line. "Where'd he get my keys? Where is he?"

"I didn't need your keys. We're a portable car wash company. We come to you."

"Today? As cold as it is?"

The man handed Carmen the receipt and quickly turned to walk away.

"Thanks for your business." He replied in habitual manner.

"Wait a second. You come to me? Do you have a card

or something?"

"The number is on your receipt," the man shouted as he ran towards the truck.

Carmen stuck her head out of the door.

"This six, one, nine, two, fffff –"

An ice cold breeze stole the words from Carmen's mouth as it scolded her and reminded her to dress appropriately when in it's presence. Carmen ducked back into the door and shook herself warm. Just as she was about to sit down the doorbell rang.

Ding. Dong.

"What could be that important for him to get back out of that truck?"

Carmen opened the door. A huge smile filled her face. All she could see was flowered paper. Huge flowered paper.

"Delivery for Carmen Trenton."

"Come on in." Carmen said as she heard the wind yell. She stood back as far as she could and attempted to hold the door with her pointer and middle finger. She knew that her assistance wasn't helping at all but she dared not challenge the wind again.

The woman worked her way through the door. She set the huge bouquet of flowers in the middle of the small hall, then put the clipboard in Carmen's direction without ever looking at her.

Carmen smiled as she signed her name. *Flowers. How nice?* She thought.

The woman took the clipboard, rolled her eyes and without saying a word, she left.

"What is Marcus doing?" Carmen smiled. She ripped

the paper off and searched for the card. She noticed the flowers weren't as big as they'd appeared. The paper was big but the flowers were small – so much so that they scarcely filled the little vase.

"That's okay, Chuggar. It's the thought that counts. Check you out! Do yo thang baby." Carmen spoke as if someone was there to hear. She smiled again. Then the phone rang.

"H-e-l-l-o." Carmen sang melodramatically.

"Look under the toaster in the kitchen." The voice commanded.

"Hey, Marcus! Thanks for the flowers... and the car wash. You are the sweetest..."

Click!

"Hello? Marcus? Hello." Carmen looked puzzled.

"I know he didn't hang up the phone."

Carmen walked towards the counter. She lifted the toaster and found the envelope. It was a crisp white envelope with gold fancy lettering. She held it in her hand for a moment as she tried to recall where she'd seen that design, that style lettering, that crisp white envelope. When she finally opened it the image of the drop of honey was a dead give away. She read the flat, rectangular card. Then she read it again. She sat down – not in a chair – she sat right there on the cold, hard ceramic floor, folded her legs like an obedient kindergarten student and read the card again.

Carmen sat there for a few moments. She stared at the floor. She stared at the red spot near the bottom of the cabinet. That was courtesy of Tyson and his new passion for making smoothies. She had given Tyson strict instructions to clean up his mess completely. Something told her he cleaned to fast. He couldn't have gotten all the strawberry-banana drippings. But who cared? There was no time to worry about that. She had to get showered, dressed and downtown by ten. It was already nine. She knew it because she could hear the sound of Oprah coming from her bedroom.

"This is BIG!" Oprah said.

"No shit Oprah. This *is* big."

Carmen jumped to her feet. She reached her hands high above her head and stretched her body. She held the position for nearly half a minute while she absorbed the scent of the flowers and the freshness of the morning. She arched her back a little further until she felt the pull run from her fingers down her arms and finally through her spine. She let out a deep breath, dropped her arms and took off running up the stairs.

She conquered the stairs two at a time. There wasn't a moment to spare. This was one time she'd be on time.

About twenty-five minutes later Carmen snatched her purse from the top of her dresser and rushed to get her keys from the hook on the wall by the back door. Instinctively she reached for keys. She couldn't believe it! Another damn card! Taped to the wall and the hook.

"Oh shit Marcus! This is too much."

It was a piece of white cardboard cut into the shape of a heart.

*'Just want to show you that I know what **love is**.*
Have a good day'

Love Always, Marcus

27

Honey Child

Carmen wiggled her toes in and out of the sudsy water. She watched carefully. She didn't want the water to spill over the sides of the large wooden bowl. It was an old looking bowl. Not ragged, just ancient looking. It looked like something that could have been hand crafted by the Mayan people she'd met years ago at the market at Chichen Itza in Mexico.

A woman dressed in all black gracefully approached her.

"How is that? Is that okay?" The woman spoke slowly. She paused after each question and looked into Carmen's face as if she expected an answer. As if she really cared. Carmen was comforted by the woman's authenticity. This was why she loved spas. For Carmen it wasn't about skin or hydrating or exfoliating. It was about relieving and renewing, herself.

"It's fine. Is there sea breeze or something in the water? It feels refreshing."

"It's a peppermint soak." The woman smiled again as she kneeled and lifted Carmen's right foot from the water. She carefully and thoroughly dried the foot, leg and each toe.

"In just a moment we're going to get you started with your Honey Do Drench. That's an excellent choice. You'll enjoy it. First your body will be bathed with a honeysuckle glycerin soap. Then I'll apply a honey and oatmeal scrub which will be buffed off with a towel."

Satisfied that she'd patted every drop of water from Carmen's right foot, the woman slid a plastic honey-colored slipper over Carmen's toes and snugly onto her foot.

Carmen thought to herself. Honey-colored slippers? I don't remember honey-colored slippers the last time I could afford to come here. Naw. They didn't have honey-colored slippers on my birthday. I know they didn't. I would have remembered that. Carmen was thoroughly impressed with the colored slippers. They've covered every detail in honey. Even the aesthician is honey tone. *'Honey Child'* is right! That's the perfect name for this place. I love places with well coordinated themes. Marcus outdid himself on this one. This was just what I needed. I can't believe this day.

"What did you say your name was?" Carmen asked the woman.

"Santha."

Once again the woman smiled. She took her time. Nothing was rushed. It was as if she had all day to be as accommodating as she possibly could or as accommodating as Carmen possibly needed. She continued explaining the procedure as she lifted Carmen's left foot from the water and began to dry it.

"After the honey and oatmeal scrub is removed, a honeysuckle balm body cream will be applied. Then your hands, feet and elbows will be wrapped in paraffin. The final step is to wrap your entire body in a spa cocoon. This helps the cream to penetrate. It leaves your skin unbelievably soft. You'll be wrapped for 20-25 minutes. During this time you can have a light honey oil scalp massage, a half hour mini-facial or a hot stone facial massage. Whichever you like."

The woman placed the other slipper on Carmen's left foot then stood up and took Carmen's arm and helped her to stand. She led Carmen to the treatment room. It was all white. Crisp white like the envelope the gift certificate came in. There was soft natural sound being played throughout the spa. The sounds shifted between bird sounds and the sound of cascading water.

Carmen removed her robe and lied down on the table. Then she reached over and grabbed the book she'd been reading.

"Do you have anything I can prop this on so that I can read it while I'm getting my treatment?"

"Are you sure you want to do that? I don't have anything in here to put it on but I can find something if you absolutely must read it." The woman said.

"Would you please? I'm starting up a new class at church next week and I'm getting married tomorrow so I may not get another chance to read it. I have to read it to make sure it's okay for the teenage girls I'll be teaching."

"Oh! Congratulations!"

"Thanks. I'm so excited. I was forced out of the class a while ago. I absolutely love teaching and sharing with young people or just people in general. Now since I'm getting married they've asked me -"

Carmen laughed. "You're talking about the m-a-r-r-i-a-g-e."

The woman laughed. "Yes. The big day."

"Yeah. Thanks." Carmen smiled and began reading the book – '*Mama's Notes*'.

28

Ass Backwards

"Rise and Shine, Ms. Thang. Today is the big day."

Sharon pulled the blanket off of Carmen's head, then walked over and opened the blinds. The sunshine rushed right in and commenced to kissing Carmen's exposed skin.

Carmen shielded her eyes with her hand as she squinted trying to bring into focus the image standing beside her bed.

"Let's go! Rise and shine. You don't think you can just lay in bed all day, do you? This is one thing you will be on time for."

Recognizing the voice of the person speaking to her, Carmen rested her hand, totally covering her eyes.

"Are we alone?," she grunted.

"As far as I can see," Sharon replied as she pretended to look around the room.

"I need a test."

"What?"

"I did the gardener."

"Did the gardener? What gardener? You don't have a gardener, Hun. Have you been dreaming again?"

"The delivery guy."

Carmen spoke in a deep raspy voice as she rubbed her eyes.

"Who? Barney?" Sharon's voice was filled with shock and disbelief.

She lowered her butt to the bed slowly. She sat still with her eyes towards the dresser on the opposite side of the room. Anywhere but towards Carmen. She did not want to be looking at Carmen when she heard the answer to her question.

Carmen didn't answer.

"Carmen, are you talking about Barney?" Sharon asked.

"I need a test."

"When? You did him when?"

"Yep."

"When, Carmen?"

"Last night." Carmen answered as if she herself couldn't believe what had occurred.

"Four times." She added as she slowly shook her head side to side. "I need a test."

"Last night?!"

"Yes."

"Did you forget you are getting married tonight?"

It was a rhetorical question. The room was silent for a few moments.

Carmen finally spoke.

"I need a test." She repeated a fourth time.

"Girl, c'mon, get up. We've got to get you ready."

"Did you hear me?" Carmen asked.

"No, and I don't want to hear you. Nobody else heard you either, so, it didn't happen. You were dreaming. I'll see to it that Barney knows it was only a dream. Get up. Today is a new day. Let's go. What do you need help with?"

Sharon was trying her best to sound perky and excited.

"I need three to six months. I need a test. It takes three to six months to show up, right?"

"Aw, hell! Are you talking about an HIV test? I thought you were talking baby. You think Barney has AIDS? Did he tell you that? Did he have sores or something? What? Why do you think he has AIDS?" Sharon was frantic.

"I don't." Carmen responded slowly. "But I have to be sure."

"Sugar why didn't you make him wear a hat?" Sharon's voice was filled with confusion.

"It wasn't supposed to happen."

"Four times?! He fell in it four times?"

Carmen was silent.

"Why now, Carmen? After all this time you've known him. Had you been drinking or something?"

"Yeah, but... I like him."

"You've always liked him but not like that. At least that's what you said."

Carmen's body language filled in the silent gaps. She lay still in fetal position in the center of the bed. Her face was tucked beneath her arm. She wanted to disappear. She felt her world spinning around her. It was as if a tornado was pulling, sucking her into it's core. A black hole. She tucked herself, diminishing her size so that she'd fit. She was tired... mentally, physically... just tired. Even her tone of voice was unusual.

"I don't know, Sharon. I don't know."

"Well I know. That was, what it was. Sex. That's all sweetie."

Please don't call me 'sweetie,' Carmen thought to herself as she related to words once spoken by Spring.

"I need a test. Men can leak the whole time. He didn't do it in me, you know what I'm saying, but that uhmm... pre-cum."

She half blurted the word pre-cum as she again heard Spring's voice in her head.

"He could have got me with that."

She shook her head again from side to side.

"I messed up. I don't know. I don't know."

"Carmen, this is not that big of a deal. You screwed up. Okay. Life goes on. What Marcus doesn't know won't hurt him. Better now than later. Shake it off. Technically, you were still a free woman."

"I was doing so well. Done with Boston, Ace, Tyrone... all of em filed away. Then Barney slips in and throws everything off. Everything's up for grabs. How can I know that this won't happen again?"

Carmen rambled, speaking more to herself than to Sharon.

Sharon sighed.

"You'll be okay. It was just sex. Just one time. Well, four times..."

Sharon hesitated as she tried to remember the last time she'd been so lucky.

"But, it still classifies as one incident. And that's nothing. Well, it's something..."

Sharon fought hard to suppress the visual her mind was forming. The passion. Four times in one night, with one man! Good gracious, she thought to herself. That was just the sort of guy she was looking for. Sharon's mind was racing. She'd have to be a little nicer to her own UPS guy and the mailman too.

"But the difference is, you love Marcus."

"I love Barney right now."

Carmen's words were stiff and empty.

"You can't compare that to you and Marcus."

"Yes, Sharon, I can."

"How? You haven't built anything with Barney. It was just sex. You don't love Barney! Barney is just a nice guy and you just had a weak moment."

Carmen didn't respond.

Sharon continued. "I know he does special favors for you, packing and labeling your shipments for you, and he goes to extra lengths to deliver your packages but that doesn't make him The One. You don't love Barney! Don't get this twisted! Barney is just a nice helpful guy just like many other nice helpful guys you know. Love has nothing to do with it!"

"I know. That's the problem." Carmen said.

Sharon was speechless.

She got it. She knew Carmen well and fully understood her. Her last few words were crystal clear. Carmen did not love Barney. Nope. But more importantly, Sharon now knew Carmen didn't love Marcus either. Sharon was without words. What could she say to that? Truth was, Sharon had been so happy that Carmen was focusing on something other than Spring, that she hadn't questioned Carmen's relationship with Marcus. Plus,

Carmen was finally disconnecting herself from the trilogy: Tyrone, Ace and Boston. That fact alone was grounds for approval of Marcus.

"So what did he deliver anyway?" Sharon attempted to change the conversation.

"Clarity." Carmen replied.

This isn't going well, Sharon thought to herself. She realized she needed to clear the air of the reality of Carmen's last few statements, which hovered like cumulus clouds threatening to rain on the parade.

"This house is a mini mess. I know you like everything natural and all, but it isn't everyday that my best friend, my homie, my road dog, gets to paint herself a new life with a special man who *loves her dearly*."

Sharon smiled as she picked up the phone and began dialing.

"I'm gonna get some of the ladies over here to help me transform this place."

After their meeting the other night, Sharon totally forgot she'd decided she was done with those ladies, The Beautiful Ones.

"We're celebrating new beginnings over here and I say we get this party started!"

Sharon words spilled out quickly with as much manufactured enthusiasm as she could manage.

Carmen grabbed the covers and pulled them over her head. She needed something to shield her from Sharon's love. It was too much to handle. Carmen needed time alone. She needed to talk to Spring. She'd spent hours trying to feel her. How she missed Spring. How she needed Spring. Spring would know what to do. She had a way of cutting through the bull and the facade. She'd dig right to the core, smack dab in the middle of truth. Where was Spring now? Why wouldn't she answer Carmen's pleas? Maybe Spring wasn't with her always as she had wanted to believe. Spring wouldn't sit idly by at a time like this. She'd send Carmen a memory, a word, a vibe or something to guide her. What in the hell was going on? Nothing made sense. Ace. She needed to talk to Ace. She needed to tell him some things she couldn't tell anyone else, not even Sharon. She needed to hear him tell her some things. Her mind was cluttered with guilt, shame and confusion. Ace would give it to her straight. He'd pull no punches with her. Then he'd stand by her side, hold her hand if need be, as she dealt with reality. Whatever reality might be.

Carmen's arm emerged from beneath the sheet. She stretched her body as she felt around trying to locate the phone.

"Emily is going to send her housekeeper over within the hour."

Sharon hung up the phone.

"You want some tea?"

"No, thanks." Carmen said as she grabbed the phone and pulled it towards her.

"You want something to eat?"

"No, thanks."

"You need me to do anything up here right now?"

"No, thanks."

"Well, we're going to have to get this ball rolling, somehow."

"I know. I'm going to jump in the shower in a couple of minutes. Just let me lay here for a few more minutes."

"Okay, I'm going to get started downstairs. Holler if you need me."

"Okay."

Once Carmen heard the door close, she pressed the numbers. It seemed to take less than a minute for Carmen to try all three numbers. That speed dial was really, really quick. Too quick. Carmen dialed each number again. This time she paused and listened to the messages. *He's traveled beyond... He's out of the office until Monday...* No answer. Where is he?

Thoughts raced through Carmen's mind. She had to find Ace. She couldn't proceed without having talked to Ace. She'd call Lorna, his assistant. She'd know where he was and how to get in touch with him.

Carmen grabbed her phonebook.

" L... Where is this damn number? I know it's in here. What's her last name?"

Carmen rubbed her temples slowly as she thumbed through the pages.

"Whitehead... Wilson... I know it's a W. Wotsock! Here it is."

Carmen let out a sigh of relief as she dialed the numbers.

"Leave a message?! Shit! Well Mrs. Spartan. I have no other choice..."

Ace Spartan. Only Abraham would chose to name himself Ace Spartan. Carmen hated to call his house. She knew Suzy well and she liked her, hell, she helped to pick her, but she wasn't quite comfortable calling or visiting her home.

Afterall, Carmen still loved Ace and she knew he loved her. Suzy liked Carmen. She knew that Carmen was the one woman that wasn't a threat to her marriage. Carmen knew Ace well. Ace was a player. Carmen couldn't change that. Suzy couldn't change that but the difference was, Suzy could deal with it.

Suzy earned her title, *Wife*. That's why Carmen didn't like intruding into their home. Carmen felt Suzy had the war scars and she deserved the respect that came with the title. Nevertheless, this was an emergency.

Ring. Ring.

"Hello," the woman snapped.

Carmen hesitated. She didn't recognize the voice.

"Hi. May I speak with Ace?"

"He isn't in. May I tell him who called?" The voice calmed.

"Yes, would you ask him to call Carmen."

"Carmen Trenton. Is this Carmen Trenton?" The voice was friendly now. It was Suzy. Carmen could tell.

"Yeah, is this Suzy?"

"Hey, girl! I thought that was your voice. How are you?"

"I'm cool, looking for that husband of yours. Has he been gone long? Do you expect him back soon?"

"Well you know, Ace. I think he's…"

Carmen could tell by Suzy's voice that she didn't have a clue as to where Ace was nor did she know when he'd return. Carmen didn't want Suzy to hear the, *I told you so*, in her voice so she quickly shifted the direction of the conversation.

"Or is he gone to Mars, his favorite place?"

They both laughed.

Before Suzy could answer, Carmen continued.

"How is that big boy of yours? Ace told me he's looking just like you."

"Looking like me but girl, he's acting just like him. Walks like him, talks like him, even pisses like him."

"What?"

"Yeah, he adores his daddy. He's tries to be just like him. Bull-headed and all."

"Oh, shit! Well, we'd better get him some help now. Maybe we can save him, or save us. The world ain't ready for two of them."

"You ain't never lied. I'm trying to deprogram him now. But what can I say? He looks at me with those big eyes and cracks that half smile just like Ace, and it's all over. I just melt."

"Aw, I'm going to have to bring the kids by to play with him. Anyway, I'm not going to keep you. You get back to your little Prince, but be sure to tell the King to call me as soon as you talk to him. It's rather important."

"Is, uhm, is everything alright?"

"It'll be alright as soon as I talk to that man of yours."

"Well, as soon as I hear from my husband I'll have him to call you. And I'll be praying for you. It was good hearing from you, Carmen."

"Thanks, and it was good talking to you."

Carmen slowly hung up the phone. She'll be praying for me? Carmen thought to herself. What?

Carmen waited and waited on her call from Ace, her sign

from Spring, anything. She could feel herself becoming drowsy. She wished she had the energy to get up and move those damn triangles. She'd studied them for hours the night before last when she got home from the "Success" meeting at Emily's. Now, against her will she was focusing in on them again. Her real life triangle was straying farther and farther from her model success triangle. It was depressing. Like she was on a runaway horse without possession of the reins – as a matter of fact, she was backwards facing the ass – out of control. She sunk into a pit of depression and eventually drifted to sleep. She slept for hours.

29

Happy New Year

Carmen was awakened by Sharon. It was ten minutes to eleven and her house was filled with guests. In one hour and ten minutes she would be kissed in Holy Matrimony. She should be dressed.

Carla was in the closet fiddling with Carmen's dress.

"Sandra over there at Scott's Designs knows she designs the most beautiful dresses. It was so nice of her to let you borrow this one. Carla said.

Sharon agreed. "Wasn't that nice of her? She got the shoes too. Dropped them off this morning. She gave them to Carmen as a shower gift. You know how she is. She wants everything to be perfectly coordinated. She said she didn't want anything messing up the flow of that dress. Plus she was trying to fill the *something old, something new, something borrowed, something blue.*"

"Well she outdid herself this time." Carla commended. "Boston is going to eat his heart out. He's downstairs. Sharp as a dozen daggers. Looking good!"

"A dozen daggers? Who'd you get that from? Your grandma?" Sharon joked.

Carmen didn't laugh. She didn't smile. She wasn't yet

ready to deal with people. She needed a little more time. Just a few minutes maybe.

"Ace called." Carla said casually.

"When?" Carmen was calm and nonchalant. She no longer needed to speak with Ace. She'd asked for a sign and she'd gotten it. While napping, she'd had a dream that she was old, real old, about ninety and Ace called her from Hawaii where he was with Suzy and about five children, and shitloads of grandchildren. He was explaining to her why her man wasn't good enough for her. He was telling her to just wait, God would send her someone who was right for her. She couldn't remember how the dream ended but for some reason she woke up pissed with Ace.

"About an hour ago. He said he was at the office and he heard a message from you. He said he was taking care of some business and wasn't sure he'd make it tonight but to tell you that he said 'Congratulations' and he'd call you tomorrow. Can you believe him? Your best friend and he doesn't even make it to your wedding."

Sharon looked at Carla as if to signal her to stop talking.

Carmen stood up and stretched. She took in a deep breath and then exhaled.

"I guess I'll clean this body. Marcus thinks he's getting a demo. It's our little secret that he's getting a classic."

Carmen smiled as she headed towards the bathroom. As Carmen turned on the shower, Carla stepped in the doorway.

"Who is Nicholas? Is that another of your ex-beaus? He came in right before Marcus got here. People were taking bets as to who the husband-to-be was, Boston or this Nicholas guy?

Boston was winning, until Marcus got here and made sure it was known that he was the leading man."

Carla smiled and widened her eyes.

"That damn Nicholas is looking so good, I started to tell him to give up the tux and let Marcus use it for the wedding."

Sharon walked over to Carla and grabbed her arm.

"Come on, Miss. We're trying to get her married tonight. Who's paying you, Tyrone? Let her get in the shower so we can make this midnight appointment."

"We? Who are you marrying?" Carla jokingly asked Sharon.

Carla knew exactly what she was doing. She wanted to be sure Carmen was sure. She didn't particularly care for Marcus and could not understand Carmen's attraction to him. He had too much chit-chat for Carla. He reminded her of a messy old, fussy woman. Sit on his butt and talk is all he seemed to be good for.

"Your dress and everything will be here on the bed. We'll come and get you when it's time. Okay? When you're dressed, tap on the door. Angie's gonna come in and put the finishing touches on your hair, and Tracey's gonna get your face together, you know, put the icing on the cake. And I guess that'll be that."

Carla tilted her head and looked into Carmen's eyes.

"Now, you sure you want to do this? Because you can still change your mind if you're not sure."

"Of course she's sure." Sharon said as she began pulling the bathroom door closed.

"Are you sure, Carmen? I know you can speak for yourself."

Carla slid her foot up and stopped the door from closing at about its halfway point.

Carmen smiled as she thought of Carla, her younger sister protecting her again as she always had.

"I'm okay. Really, I am."

Sharon grabbed the knob and closed the bathroom door. As they exited the room she explained. "Nicholas is just a guy Carmen met at Mr. Hickey's funeral. I think he's Mr. Hickey's nephew. He's an attorney. They're just friends."

"Well, Carmen may think they're just friends but I think ole Nicholas had other hopes. Girl, he showed up with two dozen roses and they were not addressed to Mr. And Mrs. nothing. They were for Carmen. And he gave me this envelope for her."

Carla grabbed the card from the top of the bookcase in the hallway where she'd placed it and she handed it to Sharon.

****

Carmen was in squat position, facing the toilet, a leg hugging each side. She felt she was going to be sick. Nothing came up, but she could feel it rumbling. She felt a sharp pain in her side. She didn't know if it was coming from the inside or the outside due to her girdle or body shaper as it's called. That thing was so tight. It must have shrunk her two sizes. She was probably a six or a seven in that thing. It made everything smooth. With the body shaper and those control top pantyhose, she looked twenty-three again. It was so hard to stoop in the tight squeezing stuff. She felt faint. She lowered herself onto the floor beside the toilet. She needed to stay close. She still felt the rumbling. Eleven-thirty. She had thirty minutes to pull it all together.

Stand, the song by Donnie McClurkin was playing on her CD player on the top shelf above her towel rack. Carmen pressed the *play* button right before she'd started feeling sick. She'd forgotten that she was listening to that song the other day. That song had given her strength to face the fact that she was losing her home in about a week. Carmen hadn't thought about it since. That is until now.

"Not now, Donnie," Carmen pleaded.

As she sat there alone, she began to think about everything. She thought of all her previous men and all of her friends and their men. She wondered what the answer was. Or, if there was an answer? Is this life how is supposed to go? Drama? Puzzles with missing pieces? I like him but he's selfish. He's sweet and kind but I don't like him. He's attentive but he's also a control freak. He's fine but he's dumb. He's goofy but he's rich. He makes me laugh but he's broke and he's trying to break me. Where does it end? Are people expected to just pick the lesser of evils and roll with that? Lord, there has to be an answer.

Now she was talking to God. Without intent, Carmen's thoughts and Stand stuck on repeat, led her into a conversation with the One whom she believed had all the answers. How could she have forgotten?

With her head hung in the toilet bowl, she began speaking aloud.

"Dear God, I come first praising you Lord. Please Lord, I hope I don't sound as if I'm judging you or doubting you. Lord

I know that it was you all the time. You kept me, and guided me, and made me as I am. That's why I'm coming to you Father. I don't understand. I need to hear from you, Lord. My mind is so cluttered. I don't feel right. I don't feel natural. I feel separated. Speak to me Lord. I don't hear you. I need to hear from you. I can't do this. I can't live like this Lord. Lord please forgive me for being me, a blemished soul. I can't get it right, Lord. I keep trying to do this thing and I fall flat on my face."

The song kept pressing...

Tell me, how do you handle the guilt of your past? Tell me how do you deal with the pain? ...

"Every time, I think I'm going to get there, to that place where I'm all good, I mess up. I know you are sick of me dancing with evil then looking to you to rub my swollen feet and heal my blisters. You are all I know to be true, you and my belief in you."

Carmen began to cry.

"Don't leave me now, Lord. Not when I need you most. I come to you humbled. God, I come confessing that I have sinned. I slept with this dude. Well, I know you know. I'm sorry. I don't know what it is. Help me, Lord. This sex thing..."

Carmen cried harder, short breaths and all.

Donnie sang with conviction... **You just stand.**

"Lead me and guide me, please! I want to follow you. I don't know how to be better without losing my mind. I try. I really try."

Stand. Stand. Through the storm and through the rain. Donnie insisted.

"I'm trying." Carmen cried.

"Have mercy on me. Lord, I apologize for even entertaining the thought that Ace or Spring or anyone else could provide answers for my life. You made me, You and your never changing hands. You know how much I can bear. You know why I do, what I do, when I do it. Give me clarity. Show me where You need me, how You need me to be. I'll do it. Lord, I don't want to hurt Marcus. I appreciate him. I don't think I love him as I should. But I guess I'm going to do the best I can with what I've got. Lord, grant me patience as I wait on your guidance so that I may be the wife that you would have me to be. Bless us, Lord. Teach me to respect him and to allow him to lead me. Speak Lord! I need you! Have mercy Father God. Speak to me!"

Carmen pleaded.

Donnie concluded. **You just stand.**

Just as the song ended, the bathroom door opened. Carmen was startled momentarily. It was Tysa. She was already dressed. She walked over to Carmen and hugged her.

"Are you okay, Mommy?"

"Yeah Tysa, I'm okay." Carmen replied as she wiped her face. Snot and tears blended on her cheeks.

"You look so pretty, Tysa."

"Why are you crying? Are you angry? Did you hurt yourself?"

"I'm not feeling well Tysa, but I'll be alright."

"Okay, Mom. You know what we need to do. Get up, Ma."

Tysa pulled at Carmen's arms.

"We have to do the dance."

"No, not now, Tysa. I need to get dressed. Its almost time for me to get married, baby."

"No, Mom. You have to do the dance first. You can't get married sick!"

"Okay, Tysa. Okay."

Carmen began to swing her arms side to side appeasingly, while holding Tysa's little hands. Tysa seemed unsatisfied. Carmen added slight movement of her feet. She stepped to the side then back and onto something hard that hurt. Carmen glanced towards the floor to see what she'd stepped on. The shoebox. Carmen's flat-footed dancing had landed her on top of the box of shoes Emily brought her. The side of the box was crunched down. The lid was partially off. Carmen could see the tall heel. Everything seemed okay. Nothing was broken.

Her attention was drawn back to Tysa as the images of the shoe continued to register. Tall heel. Lots of straps. Gold colored. Black tag on the top of the sole. G...?!! Carmen quickly turned to look at the box. **GOLD??!!!!!!!**

Carmen's mouth flew open. Nothing came out. Her soul stirred. She thought she might cry. She was flabbergasted. Gold shoes?! Why gold? Carmen *does not* wear gold shoes. No matter the style, the cost, the occasion nor source! What type of wicked joke was this? Carmen thought to herself. Who knew? Carmen hadn't shared Spring's gold shoes issue with anyone. She had never discussed the whole Oz, Dorothy, wizard thing with anyone but Spring.

"Wha..."

"Come on, Ma." Tysa pulled Carmen through the bedroom door out into the hallway towards the back stairs.

"Tysa. I can't go down there like this. Tysa!" Carmen exclaimed with as much authority as she could pack into a whisper.

Tysa kept on pulling.

"What did I say, Tysa!"

"We have to dance out here, in the rain. We can't do a RainDance without rain." Tysa said in her old woman's way as she opened the back door.

"Tysa, stop it! It's too cold for that, we have to wait for spring for the rain. Get back in here!"

Just then Carmen felt it. It was rain.

"Say the words ma! Say the poem! Dance!" Tysa commanded as she pulled away and ran out into the yard.

"Tysa get your butt in here."

Carmen reluctantly went out to get Tysa.

"Ma! God sent the rain! Dance, mom! Say the poem!" Tysa danced around.

Carmen conceded.

Carmen began to dance. They were all over the place. Though there was no music playing, Carmen and Tysa kept the same rhythm. It was Nature's Rain Concerto. Just like when Carmen and Spring were kids.

The wind, the moon and the trees all stood still in honor of the special performance, "Tribute To God." Mother Nature was in charge of stage production and Tysa had been called to be the choreographer. Tonight Carmen gave the performance of her life. She swung her hips to the left, stretched her arms high above her head as her feet drifted like feathers barely touching the ground. She swayed, spinned and floated through movements which were not her own.

    Tysa smiled and mimicked each motion with a grace that could be classified as heavenly. This was clearly not their dance. Not the rehearsed dance that had been used to sooth their souls on several other occasions. No, this was not about them and it was not about soothing. This was giving. Giving all they had. This was about appreciation. This was about celebration. This was about freedom.

    As she danced, Carmen could feel the shackles releasing her. She lifted her face towards the sky giving thanks, honor and praise to God as she recited Spring's poem.

Rain Dance

I am free, free as free can be
there's no need to worry about me
I've got a move
my ancestors used
guaranteed to shake loose the blues

Watch me as I shake my thang
make it rain and loose the pain
wash away fears
blend in my tears
Workin' this move
my ancestors used
guaranteed to shake loose the blues

Bobbin my head

moving my feet
flapping my arms
like I was crazy
Watch me...
I don't care if you see
cause I've got a move
my ancestors used
guaranteed to shake loose the blues

Bind my hands
I'll do the bound dance...
swaying back and forth
Gag my mouth... I'll take it south
humming old spirituals that'll turn it out
                    soul singing

You can't hold me
I'm telling you I'm free
watch me now
I'll show you how
cause I've got a move
my ancestors used
guaranteed to shake loose the blues

I'm not afraid
my debt has been paid
you can't hold me
*I was **born** free*
see me now

dancing in the clouds
trying to bring the rain
to wash away your pain
cause me... I was born free
and I inherited a move
my ancestors used
guaranteed to shake loose the blues

God sent rain. On New Years Eve in Chicago, God sent rain.

Carmen moved her head from side to side allowing the rain to wash her neck and squeeze into her bosom. Through blurred vision, cloudy skies, and midnight haze, she could see a lone star.

It twinkled.

God's wink of approval, Carmen was sure of it.

Almost instantly, the rain ceased.

Then Carmen heard Tyson's voice.

"Ma, what are you doing? I've been looking all over for that thing. You had it all the time."

Tyson slipped the ring off of Carmen's finger and onto the white string which was attached to the fluffy white pillow with the ruffled edges.

"You had it all the time."

Tyson's words rang out loud and clear in Carmen's mind.

How apropos? Carmen thought as she slid through the small space in the doorway where her mother was standing staring at her like she'd lost her mind. She never said a word. She just stared at Carmen and her dirty stockings and tight, wet, body slip.

"Can you get Tysa some dry clothes for me?"

Carmen placed Tysa's hand in Mrs. Trenton's hand and continued walking towards the living room where the guests were gathered.

As Carmen passed through the dining room Candice asked: "Do you want me to get Marcus? He's outside helping his sister's friend get her car started. Aren't you all saying your vows before midnight? You only have a few minutes! The countdown will be starting shortly."

Carmen didn't answer.

When she reached the living room, Boston met her at the arched doorway with a bottle of Cristal in his hand. Not the common $300 Cristal. Cristal Rose-Limited, $1000 per bottle.

Seeing her, Ace who had just arrived, made his way towards her toting a fifth of Hennessey.

A blanket of silence covered the room.

Carmen politely made her way over feet and legs and around the bulky flowers that sat on the short table overcrowding the room. She plopped her wet, dirty behind right on the arm of her sofa.

All eyes were on Carmen.

Sharon and Carla stood across the room watching in amazement. Carla shook her head slowly as if she couldn't believe it.

"Always lands on her feet." Carla smiled.

Sharon looked at Carla.

"I still can't believe it. Let me read that again."

Carla handed Sharon the letter which she'd gotten from

the card that came with the flowers from the already gone man, Nicholas.

12/31

Congratulations, Ms. Soon to be Mrs., Carmen.

I hope you don't mind me showing up at your Wedding Ceremony. I saw your friend, Peaches. I think that's what she said her name was. She remembered seeing us converse at my uncle's funeral and she told me about you getting married. In light of the recent events in your life, I thought this would be the perfect time to pass along a bit of information I have for you. I'll keep it short and sweet as I know you'll be desiring to savor each moment to spend with your new husband. What a lucky man he is?!

As promised, I got an opportunity to research the printing company that disappeared with your funds. To make a long story short, the company had closed, as you stated. But, the owners of that company opened a new company under a different name in a nearby suburb. By stroke of luck, I stumbled upon an advertisement which happened to list one of the owners as a contact person. The rest was simple.

Enclosed is a check for the amount of $62,843. Please be advised that by cashing this check you forfeit any and all rights to future litigation and you are recognizing said amount as a fair and equitable settlement. Excuse the jargon, simply put, I'm saying you *won't be entitled to any more money from the company (smile).*

You don't owe me anything for my services. I am happy that I could help. My uncle spoke fondly of you. He tried on several occasions to convince me to ask you out. I'm not one for blind dates and therefore wasn't interested. My loss. I have to concur with uncle Jr., you are a gem. Again, congratulations and may God bless you.

Nicholas Hickey

I'll be damned! Sharon said under her breath as she fixed her eyes on Carmen.

Just before the countdown was to begin Carmen broke the silence. She smiled and her eyes filled with joy as she began speaking. Boston stood by her side. Ace stood just behind Boston.

Carmen reached over and grabbed Boston's champagne glass.

"Dearly beloved, we are gathered here today..."

She spoke as if she was reciting the Declaration of Independence. She raised the glass and continued.

"To praise God. Somebody give God a hand clap, why don't cha."

She smiled again. The crowd obliged. Her smile got even bigger.

"Hook me up, Ace. Not too much, I'm driving. Ha-ha." Carmen laughed.

"Driving what?" Renee asked fearlessly.

"This beautiful new life God has given me."

Carmen raised her glass.

"Toast..."

As the guests busied themselves passing glasses, bottles, confused expressions and sharp one word remarks, Carmen's attention was drawn to the left side of the room, where the guests were obviously captivated with something in the kitchen. All heads were turned.

Moments were like minutes as time passed and heads were reluctantly redirected, leaving only a few hypnotized eyes stuck in the corners of their sockets unwilling to allow one iota of the anticipated soap-opera-like drama to escape unseen.

Carmen's instincts told her it wasn't a what, but a who. Marcus. What would she say? How would she say it? Where should she say it? Questions raced through her mind.

Carmen's eyes lowered and steadied themselves on her thigh. They were locked, frozen still, as was every other part of her body. Her mind had demanded a moment of silence as all efforts were given to requesting and hearing a word from God. A sudden hush of complete silence signaled - like a final breath of life when all hopes, wishes, prayers, promises and regrets are negated by the inevitable... and the voices of the angels of destiny whisper ever so sweetly, yet uncompromisingly – *Time Up.*

Carmen looked up to face her decision. She would not cry. She'd breathe. One deep breath at a time... she'd breathe.

Marcus was standing there, in the doorway. His face was a portrait, painted by the emotions and discretions of the many guests whose stares boldly invaded the core of his being. It was a portrait of confusion and despair with which Marcus was overwhelmingly uncomfortable. He stood there like a deer caught in a car's headlights, unable to save himself.

Almost instantly his thoughts switched to Carmen. Her heart... Marcus could hear it... it was wounded... it was weeping... it was calling his name.

Marcus turned to face his friend.

Nothing was said, not one word the audience could repeat. Their emotions were private. They couldn't be interpreted. It was as if they shared a secret language which could not be decoded, not even by the best of the best.

Carmen looked deep into his eyes. She hoped he could hear her. She needed him to know... she was sorry. Words couldn't capture what she was feeling. She widened her eyes to give Marcus a clearer, unobstructed view of her soul.

He saw it. He smiled a half smile and made his way across the room to her.

"What's this? Y'all trying to toast without me? Excuse me bruh."

Marcus nudged his way between Boston and Carmen. He lovingly placed his arm around her neck, then leaned down and kissed her cheek.

"Can somebody pass me a drink?" Marcus said.

"Oh, here man, take mine."

Nate handed Marcus the short glass filled with clear brown liquid.

"Can we have silence please? Carmen is going to propose a toast."

Marcus' words echoed through the already silent room.

Carmen blinked her eyes uncontrollably. She took a deep breath, raised her glass and began to speak.

"To true friendship, to new beginnings, to the Beautiful Ones…"

Carmen looked around the room as she contemplated whether or not she should engage the group in her thoughts. She was filled with gratitude. Never before had she felt so loved. When her eyes caught Rita's she paused and winked, then she continued.

"And most importantly, to God's grace."

Carmen shook her head side to side gently as she exclaimed, "That's *unmerited divine assistance* according to Webster.

She breathed.

"Undeserved."

Her eyelids/wipers cleared the way as her soul pressed on through the storm.

"I must say I concur."

She exhaled a ton of societal inhibitions, then added, "It don't get no better than that!"

Marcus stood proud as he characteristically attempted to help. "Well, don't look at us like we're crazy. Drink up."

A voice across the room humbly interrupted.

"Marcus."

Marcus and Carmen looked in the direction from which the voice came.

Candice offered no additional words, she simply pointed towards the huge clock Sharon had rented.

The seconds were running wild;13, 12, 11…

Carmen chimed in… "Ten, Nine…"

Marcus understood the implication, yet he followed Carmen's lead.

" Eight …"

The crowd, left without option, staggered in –

"Seven, six, five." By "four," everyone was yelling in unison.

"Three, two, one – Happy New Year!"

The crowd cheered. Lovers kissed. Friends and family hugged. Children danced and jumped around blowing and swinging noisemakers. Marcus, Boston and Ace all sipped on their drinks. Tyrone emerged from somewhere, picked up Tysa and gave Tyson a soul-brother handshake and tight squeeze. And Carmen?…

Carmen simply looked towards the ceiling and whispered softly, "Amen."

She sat motionless for a few moments allowing her soul celebration. She was proud to be Carmen. All by herself - Carmen. The storm was behind her. The sun was shining in the land of Carmen's Soul. There was a guiding light. She could see the open road. She smiled. She thanked God. She pressed on.

A single tear escaped her right eye signifying all was well… Her debt had been satisfied. Glory to God.

30

For Sentimental Reasons

The music began to play.

I love you, I love you, I love you, I love you, I love you...

Sam Cooke – **For Sentimental Reasons.**

I love you... for sentimental reasons. I hope you do believe me. I've given you my, my, my, my, my, my... given you my heart. Because I... mmmm you. And you alone were meant for me. Please give your loving heart to me, and say we'll never part. I think of you every morning. I dream of you every, every, every, every night. I'm never lonely -whenever you are in sight. I know, I know, I know I love, love, love, love, love you. And you alone were meant for me. Please give your loving, loving, loving, loving, loving heart to me and tell me we'll never part...

Carmen's arm rested across her own waist. Her fingers gently tapped the softness of her stomach. Her other arm lifted into the air and out to her side in L-shaped format as she worked her way around the room. Her fingers snapped in a timely manner as if written into the notes of the song. She stiff-legged a couple of steps sort of like a waltz. Then she smooth dipped and lifted her legs occasionally bending them at the knees as only a seasoned two-stepper could. *Waltz – two-step... waltz – two-step – bop... two-step – waltz – bop – bop – bop – waltz – waltz*

– *two-step*. There was no apparent pattern to her movement yet it flowed. Carmen trusted her instincts. She moved as if no one watched. She tried it and it flowed. It flowed because she believed...

"I think of you every morning. Dream of you every..."
The chorus supported Sam as he crooned in honor of the new day.

DON'T MISS!!

Smiling Eyes
~Moments with Spring Sumner Reign~

Companion book to The Beautiful Ones. This collection of poems is taken from the mind, heart and soul of the character Spring. If you enjoyed the novel you must experience this book! Excerpts from the book:

Smiling Eyes

I see the daisy in a field of weeds
I wish I could fill everyone's needs
I enjoy dancing half-naked in the mirror with me
ninety percent of the time I'm free
Me and my smiling eyes

I see the rainbow in the midst of a storm
I pick up roses despite the thorns
I celebrate things others mourn
The Angels rejoiced the day I was born
Me and my smiling eyes

I like to take one day at a time
I'm simple minded, I like poetry that rhymes
I smile at my reflection and think damn girl, you're fine
To negative things, I'm partially blind
Me and my smiling eyes

I don't usually cry about bills
I understand that excess kills
Love is the only thing I'll leave in my will
with occasional memories to give you thrills...courtesy of

Me and my smiling eyes

~Peace........

OUT!

I once loved a handsome man,
with big hands
he offered no commitment, nor future plans

with big feet,
no place to stay, nor food to eat
he was sexy, romantic and extremely sweet

Can't recall where I put him...

Kim L. Dulaney lives in Chicago, Illinois with her two children. She is currently working on a new novel, "A Pot To Piss In..." She is also finishing her first book for teens "Mama's Notes."

Other books by this author:

Smiling Eyes
Woman To Woman
I Love Me!
My Best
Who Am I?
Maya's Magic
Kool...Kool... Kendel
My Lost Dream
I Can Fly (The R. Kelly Story)

visit Kim L. Dulaney online @
www.README4.com